A *CRACK* IN THE WALL

A CRACK IN THE WALL

Short Stories
by
Betty Jane Hegerat

for story lovers

Betty Jane

OOLICHAN BOOKS
LANTZVILLE, BRITISH COLUMBIA, CANADA
2008

Library and Archives Canada Cataloguing in Publication

Hegerat, Betty Jane, 1948-
A crack in the wall / Betty Jane Hegerat.

Short stories.
ISBN 978-0-88982-240-5

I. Title.

PS8615.E325C73 2008   C813'.6   'C2007-907671-8

We gratefully acknowledge the financial support of the Canada
Council for the Arts, the British Columbia Arts Council through
the BC Ministry of Tourism, Small Business and Culture, and the
Government of Canada through the Book Publishing Industry
Development Program, for our publishing activities.

Published by
Oolichan Books
P.O. Box 10, Lantzville
British Columbia, Canada
V0R 2H0
www.oolichan.com

Printed in Canada

This book is dedicated to the memories
of my mom and dad
Martha and Morris Harke
who taught me to be still and listen

ACKNOWLEDGEMENTS

To my family, always: Robert, Elisabeth, Eric, and Stefan who are my real life. My love and my gratitude for putting up with my absences and distractions in the years of gathering these stories. Love and thanks to Sharon, for being the very best of sisters.

To my friends: I am blessed. You share your stories and you enrich my life.

To teachers and mentors: Dave Margoshes, for teaching me that stories have a heart, and for providing open-heart surgery as required. And of course, for friendship. The Sage Hill Writing Experience and David Carpenter for allowing me to bring some of these stories to that magical place.

To Oolichan Books: for giving these stories such a fine home.

Some of these stories have appeared previously: "The Way She Ate Oranges" and "A Practical Woman" in *Grain*; "From a Stranger" in *Forum* (The Calgary Women's Writing Project); "Birdwatching" in *Grove*; "Stitches" in *Wascana Review*; "Leftovers" in an earlier version in *Storyteller*, and *Ottawa at Home* and produced and broadcast by CBC radio; "Burned" in *Pottersfield Portfolio*; "Storm Warning" and "Pockets" in *Alberta Views*; "Pins and Needles" on CBC radio's Alberta Anthology and in *The Alexandra Reader 25th Anniversary Edition* (Alexandra Writers Centre Society 2007).

I acknowledge with thanks the financial assistance of the Alberta Foundation for the Arts in the writing of the final drafts of these stories.

CONTENTS

A PRACTICAL WOMAN

The old cat hunkers on the counter next to the aquarium, more interested in the bloated goldfish now than when it was alive. Moira scoops out the fish, walks toward the kitchen garbage, shakes her head. She leaves the dripping net on the drain board and picks up the phone. The cat noses the fish through the mesh but doesn't sustain his curiosity or his appetite long enough to persist.

"Time to get down, Steps." Moira hooks an arm under his belly and lowers him to the floor, taking care to let him down gently. She winces every time he jumps off a chair, feeling the jolt in her own arthritic knee.

She turns her attention to the phone. On the fourth ring, her youngest son answers.

"Nugget died," she says.

"What?"

"Don't say 'what' to your mother." (She's been telling them this since they started to talk.)

He laughs. "Yeah, okay. Pardon, Mom?"

"Your goldfish died. Nugget. Do you want the tank or should I put it out with the trash? And how did we dispose of all the other fishy corpses?"

"I guess we flushed them. Nugget isn't mine. Mine's the catfish. The guy who lives under the bridge."

The catfish? Moira peers through the algae-coated wall of the tank. Equally scummed with green, there is a little ceramic bridge resting on a bed of gravel and under the bridge a long black shadow lurks.

"Mom? Are you there?"

"We have never flushed a pet. What should I do with the catfish? I'm leaving next week."

"I still vote toilet. He hasn't moved in years. When do you think you'll be back?"

No matter how often Moira tells the kids she's leaving for good, they don't believe her. "But this is home," they say. Home to them, but she's never felt settled out here. Even though she was the one who wanted to pack up three babies and move to Alberta all those years ago. Better jobs, better life for the kids, she'd coaxed her dubious husband. She was right about everything except him. But now that the kids are gone, she has no reason for living here.

"Hey, Mom! Are you still there? What about the rest of the zoo?" He sounds curious but not the least bit concerned.

"I'm working on that. Talk to you later."

She's already given away the garden tools, so she chips at the soil near the back gate with a rusty serving spoon. Probably a good idea to warn the landlord about the pet cemetery in case the new tenant is a gardener. One large dog buried deep and safe, two cats, rabbits without number, gerbils, hamsters. She imagines the back lane cordoned off, the entire yard turfed over, men in coveralls sifting, dropping bone fragments into Ziploc baggies.

She's wrapped the fish in an envelope of waxed paper. She lays it in the shallow bowl of earth and strategically spreads lumps of dirt. Dissatisfied with the coverage, she decides to finish the job with a layer of cat litter.

The box is over-due for a cleaning. She can smell it as soon as she walks down the basement stairs. Steps, now asleep on a piece of old carpet beside the furnace, opens one eye when he hears her scraping in his box.

"Go back to sleep," she says. "I'll worry about you later."

"I thought I'd better let you know that I'm giving Sookie to the woman at the bakery".

The little dog is asleep on her blanket, but opens black marble eyes when she hears her name announced to the daughter's answering machine.

"What?" There's a click and the familiar voice interrupts her recording. So like her own voice, it always takes Moira by surprise. "Mom? What are you talking about?"

"So you are there after all?"

"Of course I'm here. Is this some kind of a sick joke, saying you're giving my dog away just to get my attention?"

Moira holds the phone away from her ear and Sookie bounds off the couch, skittering across the bare hardwood.

"I'm leaving for Moncton at the end of the week. It'll be too hard to find a place that takes pets, and I can't drive across the country with this menagerie anyway." She picks up the dog with her free hand, hoping the snuffly whimpers will carry all the way to Toronto. "That woman who's been at the bakery for years, you know the one with the birthmark? Her Shih Tzu died this winter and she was heartbroken."

"You're giving my dog to a stranger?"

"You're welcome to fly out and get her," Moira says. Doesn't mention that she'll be stopping overnight in Toronto. She's already decided that if there are too many tears, she'll bring the dog. She hasn't really spoken to the bakery woman yet.

"You know I can't do that. I'd have to move. Do you know how hard that is in this city? You expect me to find another apartment because you're tired of looking after Sookie?"

"Just plain tired. Let me know by tomorrow night if you change your mind. Do you remember who the goldfish belongs to?"

"The what?"

"The goldfish. Nugget."

"I didn't know we had fish. The turtles were mine. I don't have room for a fish tank. Have to run, Mom. Kiss Sookie goodbye for me."

Moira hangs up and stares into the dog's pug face. Just like that. If she'd known it would be easy she would have shed this one three years ago when the daughter moved out. Sookie has never liked Moira and the feeling is mutual. Goodbye, snooty little dog.

Next, a call to the animal shelter to ask if they take birds.

"What kind of bird, Ma'am?"

"Lovebird."

"Pair?'"

"No. Single." She doesn't report that Tony the lovebird has had three mates, all of them mysteriously dead within a month. That the pet store has repeatedly said Tony would never survive as a widower and yet here he is fifteen years later.

"Sometimes," the cautious voice says, "we can place them. Especially if it's a young bird, friendly. Is he hand-trained? Can he talk?"

Already this is a lost cause. Talk? No. He shrieks. When the house is quiet he screeches until she turns on the television or the radio or opens the cage and lets him cruise. Tony hates children and is selective even with adults. A good judge of character, the kids said when the bird tried to take a chunk out of the chin of one of the few men Moira dated in the fifteen years after their dad split.

Her children had pooled their money the first Mother's Day without their dad. Too young to appreciate the irony of giving their single mother a pair of lovebirds, they hatched their plan in the conservatory at the zoo. Really, Moira hadn't even noticed what she was looking at until they pointed. "Do you like those birds?" they wanted to know.

She shrugged. "Sure. They're cute."

This was the way every animal except Steps came into their lives. "Do you like rabbits, Mom?"

"Sure. They're cute." Then a quick scurry to the back

13

step and the child would be back with a rescued bunny in his arms.

It's years since Moira's been to the zoo. She phones her eldest son, remembering that he took the kids to see the baby giraffe the last time they were here visiting.

"I don't suppose you'd want Tony," she says.

"As in Tony the psycho lovebird? Not likely. I'd prefer your grandkids to grow up with all their fingers."

"Do they still have birds in the conservatory at the zoo?"

"I don't know," he says. "We spent all our time at the snack bar."

Steps weaves a wobbly path to Moira's chair when she sits down to watch the news. She scoops the cat onto her lap and runs her hand over his greasy coat.

"He's losing interest in grooming himself," the vet said last year. And that reminds her that she forgot to crush the thyroid medication into the cat food this morning. Easing the warm burden from her knees, she goes into the kitchen for a bowl, opens the freezer for the ice cream, and stirs the tiny tablet into a melting puddle.

"Treat time, Steps. I don't have many goodies left for you."

When Steps has finished licking the bowl, Moira reaches down and then cradles the cat in her arms. Sookie springs off her own chair on the other side of the room and gambols over to claim a share of the attention.

In the kitchen, Tony has begun to squawk. Time

to throw the cover on his cage. The air pump in the aquarium burbles away.

"I'll get rid of the rest of the gang tomorrow," Moira whispers to the cat, "and we'll have a bit of peace."

She scrubs the fish tank, washes the gravel, and sets the whole kit out in the back lane beside the garbage can. FREE says the note she tapes to the side. HELP YOUR-SELF.

This has worked for countless items over the years. After Moira's husband hopped a bus one morning in-stead of going to work, and she found out he'd gone "home", back east to his old job, old life, she'd hung his suits on the rails of the fence, and let the kids set up a table and sell his books and records. Recycling. She's good at shedding possessions responsibly. A practical woman.

Moira gets into the car with the catfish in his mar-garine container of smelly water. The creek is a short drive away.

She steps into the muddy weeds and tips the fish to freedom. When he sinks in the shallows and winds himself into the shadow of a rock, she turns and walks away, taking the plastic tub home to the recycling bin.

The bakery woman is waiting in front of Moira's house when she drives up. The woman's smile slices through the deep wine stain on her cheek. "I know I'm early, but I couldn't wait," she says and then blinks and looks away. "I guess I was afraid you might change your mind."

Sookie skitters to the door to meet them, and when

the woman kneels, the little dog scrambles into her arms as though she's been waiting all her life for this saviour.

The tattered blue blanket, the bag of toys, a case of dog food, and the stainless steel bowls are all stashed in the woman's little car. When she's driven away, the house seems cold and very still.

Moira turns on the radio, and sets the kettle to make tea. Steps wanders into the kitchen. From the remnants of the pantry now packed in two boxes on the counter, Moira scrounges sardines. The cat waits patiently, leaning against Moira's ankle while she unfurls the top of the can and lays one oily fish on a saucer. She'll save the rest to have on toast. "Fresh fish back home, Kitty," she says. "Lobster, the first night in." The cat coughs, and retches up the half-chewed sardine. Moira phones the vet and makes an appointment two days away.

Eldest son calls home that night, offering to come out and help her pack. "Have you booked a van, Mom?"

Moira reaches across the bedroom floor to drag the phone closer. Because she'd been asleep for more than an hour when the phone rang, it takes her a minute to collect her thoughts. The room is empty except for the mattress, and the suitcases and boxes along the wall.

"No van," she tells him. "I'm traveling light. I won't need any help. But I'll stop for a quick visit." She's already planned an overnight stay in Regina. Always a pleasure to share her grandsons' room so they can giggle together in the bottom bunk.

"I'm nervous for you, Mom, but glad too. We'll come out for Christmas this year."

16

He's been making regular trips to the east coast for years, this boy. The only one of the three who's forgiven their dad for bailing, and visits with him as well as with aunts and uncles and cousins on both sides.

"Hey, it sounds like you're sweeping the nest clean. What are you doing about Steps?" he asks.

Moira looks to the end of the bed where the old cat is nested in the folds of her velour housecoat. Steps belongs to all of the kids, the third cat they acquired after two short-lived kittens. Their dad went out early the morning after they'd chipped a hole in the half-frozen November garden to bury cat number two. When he came back the older kids were at the table, the youngest in his high chair, all staring glumly into bowls of Cheerios. He pulled a bedraggled kitten from his pocket. "Look what I found on the back steps," he said.

"Mom? Are you there? Do you want to leave Steps with us?"

She shakes her head. Her daughter-in-law has asthma. The cat looks up with one eye, the other caked with pus. Moira needs to press a warm cloth to it every morning. "No," she says, "I couldn't do that."

Youngest son phones ten minutes later when she's in the kitchen eating toast and sardines. She's mashed the fish for Steps this time and lifted him to the counter where he crouches in front of her, scarfing up the snack, one eye on the dish and the crusted one on her, unable to believe this indulgence.

"Hi, Mom. Sorry to call so late. I always forget about the hour's difference."

He offers to fly home on the weekend. To help her get away. They're such fine boys, Moira thinks, staring

17

into the dark beyond the kitchen window, the smell of fish oiling the back of her throat.

"Honestly, I don't need any help," she tells him. She wishes he was also on her route, but Vancouver is the opposite direction. "Fly out at Christmas instead. I'm hoping all of you will come." She's sure they will. Their older brother will convince them and probably convince them to visit their dad as well. If they haven't already. Moira never asks.

"What are you going to do out there, Mom? You're way too young to retire." And too poor but she doesn't remind him of this.

"Nurses are in short supply everywhere. I've already lined up some interviews."

The phone doesn't have a chance to cool before it shrills again. She's sure it's her daughter, but instead another familiar voice hits her like a big dog to the back of her knees. She clutches the counter.

"Hello? Moira? Are you still there?"

"Yeah." She hoists herself onto the counter, one foot braced against the sink.

"I hear you're coming back."

His voice hasn't changed. In fact it's deeper and more mellow than it was in the last phone call when she told him she never wanted to hear from him again. "Finally quit smoking, eh?"

He laughs. "How can you tell? You're too far away to smell my clothes."

"Your voice," she says. "I figured you'd sound like your dad by now."

"Nah, after the heart attack I decided I didn't have any choice. You knew I had heart trouble a few years back?"

18

So she'd heard, from their eldest. At the time, she wished he'd die. Hearing his voice again, she's probably glad he didn't. "No," she lies. "And I guess I don't need to hear about it now. What do you want?"

"Lord God Almighty, you haven't changed a bit. I wanted to tell you I'm glad you're coming back. I know you hate it out there even though you're too stubborn to admit it."

"Look, I have a lot to do here. Packing and getting rid of all these damn pets."

"Yeah, I guess you do. Why don't you call me when you get in?"

"Why would I want to do that?" Steps has wandered into the kitchen looking dazed and stares up at her as though he'd give anything to make the leap to the counter. But he can't. Instead, he yowls.

"What the hell is that?"

"The cat. One of the many responsibilities you walked out on."

"The same old cat? What was his name again? Steps, right? Still alive after all these years?"

"Barely," she says. She slides off the counter and strokes Steps' lumpy fur. He stops howling, winds himself around her leg, his purring rough and mucousy.

"Aw, you're not planning on doing away with Steps before you leave? Christ, if he's lived this long he'll make it another three thousand miles. Bring him along. I'll take him."

She feels such a rush of rage, she growls into the phone. "How dare you offer to help now. You dumped me when I needed you most!"

She hangs up the phone and sits a long while, cry-

19

ing, with the trusting weight of the cat leaning warm against her shin.

Finally she's aware of Tony keening. Never has she heard him mimic so well. She opens the cage door and lets him perch on her shoulder where he bobs his head, regurgitating seed, trying to deposit it in her ear. He's never needed another Cleo. She's been enough for this feathery little Anthony.

Moira's is one of the first cars into the zoo parking lot. Only a few moms pushing strollers full of early-rising babies and toddlers make their way to the entrance. The landscape has changed since she was last here. There's a new entrance, and the skeleton of a massive new construction rises over the old buildings. But still she can see the conservatory flanked by flower beds mulched and ready for snow.

Tony is on the passenger seat in a hamster cage salvaged from the last of the boxes she piled on the front step this morning for the Goodwill pick-up. After screeching all the way, when the car stops Tony is suddenly silent and huddles into the corner of the cage, trembling.

Moira lifts him out, holds his little body in front of her nose and he tilts his head to stare at her. Such an exotic treasure with his peach-coloured face, the fan of turquoise tail against the moss green of his body. He feels like velvet when she brings him to her cheek.

Fortunately, he's always loved to hide in pockets.

By the time she walks to the conservatory, pushes through the protective double entry that keeps the birds in, the weather out, he's twitching and starting to squawk. There are two young people in uniforms leaning against the counter at the snack bar and one little family on the path. Tony's calls blend with the chitter of rainbow birds flitting through the lush greenery.

Moira faces the waterfall in the farthest corner from the snack bar and waits until a little boy who's trying desperately to wet his chubby hand has gone back to his mother.

She lifts Tony out of her pocket, his heart pounding against her palm, and hides him against the front of her jacket. When she relaxes her fingers, he stays cupped in her hand. Even when she gently slides the hand away, he clings to her lapel. But then, a small orange bird lights in the hibiscus in front of her and in a flash of green Tony is gone, blending perfectly into the tropical forest. Knowing that it's only a matter of time before he returns to her shoulder, she leaves quickly, and doesn't look back.

While Moira packs the car and sweeps the house clean, Steps sits in the middle of the kitchen looking confused. His head swivels from side to side, following her progress. Finally, she makes one last circuit of the empty rooms, and picks up the cat. She wishes she had a carrier today. For years they put Steps in a pillowcase for trips to the vet. They discovered by accident that he stayed oddly quiet if he was bundled blind and held tightly. The last time, he was too sick to care and she laid him in the front seat.

The cat stiffens when Moira opens the car door and almost springs from her arms before she can slide inside. When the door is closed she lets go, and he leaps from her arms to the floor in the back and cowers there, howling.

Fortunately, it's a short drive to the animal clinic, but it takes Moira five minutes to coax Steps out from under the seat. The waiting room is packed. One look at Moira's face, a glance at the appointment schedule, and the receptionist takes her through to an empty examining room. By the time the vet comes in, the cat is calmed in her arms, but clawing tight to the front of her sweater.

"Well if isn't my old friend, Steps."

She's pleased they've drawn the most senior of the doctors today. A soft-hearted Scotsman who miraculously pulled Steps through distemper a week after he was "found" on the back steps.

She swallows hard. "I'm moving," she says, and "there's no one to take him."

The vet cups a gentle hand over the cat's ears, leans close to look in his eyes. "Actually," he says quietly, "he doesn't look too bad at all. But frail, eh? And comes a time . . . "

Steps looks from one to the other of them and begins to purr.

There's a tap on the door. A phone call for the doctor. He takes Moira's elbow and steers her gently to a chair. "You just sit a minute. I won't be long."

He told her once long ago in his soft Scottish brogue that cats are his favourite animals. She nodded. Hers too.

Moira thinks about the catfish in the clear stream, Tony perched high on a bougainvillea vine, Sookie nibbling pastry treats, red bows in her freshly clipped hair. And Nugget.

She opens the door and carries Steps out to the car without waiting for the vet. He'll understand.

The pillowcase is easy to find in the suitcase of linen in the trunk. Steps goes limp when she eases him into the cloth bag and puts him on the passenger seat. Moira keeps one hand on the pillowcase while she pulls into traffic. She's sure that by the time they leave the city Steps will find his way out. It's a long journey, and he'll be good company.

PINS AND NEEDLES

Bert had just flung a shovelful of snow into the air and earned himself a flash of angina when the van pulled up across the street. Momentarily distracted, he ignored the pressure in his chest, and watched through the backdraft of swirling flakes as a skinny blonde waltzed up his neighbour's front walk. There was constant traffic through Stan and Heather's place. Tupperware or some damn thing she was involved with.

Stan's front door opened, his massive bulk framed in the doorway as he waved the blonde inside. Bert shook his head. A brand new Dodge the colour of fine claret idling away unattended. A person should look after a vehicle like that.

Bert turned and stomped to the top of the driveway. The temperature had to have dropped twenty degrees since yesterday's sticky snowfall. Two more scrapes down to the street would do it, but the snow peeled up like cement, the final heave to the pile on the lawn enough of a challenge that he knew he should have swallowed his pride and paid some kid twenty bucks to do the job.

The fist of his old enemy squeezed harder, no longer just taunting. Bert fumbled in his pocket for the vial, slipped a tablet under his tongue and waited, savouring the image of that tiny torpedo blasting through his arteries. Waited, as usual, with morbid curiosity and a rusty prayer at the ready. Although, this might not be a bad way to lose the battle—shovelling snow on a day when the path to heaven was a dazzling blue. Straight to the light. Wasn't that how they described it? All those fools who claimed to have been to death and back?

"Bert? You okay?" Lil's voice quivered in the cold.

Caught in the act. Bert tried to time himself to Lil's patrol past the living room window, make sure he was leaning on the shovel smiling every ten minutes. She'd be counting the nitro tablets in the container on his dresser tonight. He waved, and flicked the tassel on his hat. Lil had cajoled him into wearing the Santa cap in case Deb and the grandson arrived while he was outside. After grumbling the requisite number of minutes, he'd rammed it down around his ears so they stuck out like handles on a cracked sugar bowl.

"I look like some demented old elf," he grumbled. But he'd be just as tickled as Lil to see the look on little Caleb's face when he a got a load of Grandpa Santa. Kids. Bert had always been a pushover for the little guys. Lil was standing in the doorway, hugging herself to keep warm, squinting against the glare of snow.

"Still alive, Lil. See . . ." Bert exhaled, puffing out a ring of ice fog, and then he grinned. "Go on back to your paper. Check tomorrow's obits and see if I'm there."

She slammed the door, but he was sure she was smiling. He had to remind himself to keep the jokes coming, even if they were gallows humour. Yesterday Lil had come home from shopping with his prescription refill in her bag, and he'd been fresh out of funnies. "So what's the point here, Lil? What the hell point is there to me shuffling around with a time bomb under my shirt?"

She'd burst into tears and locked herself in the bathroom. By the time she slammed the sandwich down in front of him, he'd decided to keep the news about Needles to himself. At least until she stopped sniffing and looking at him with eyes like a couple of poached eggs ready to slide over the top of her glasses.

As soon as he was done the walks he'd go in and show her the stark little block of print in yesterday's *Herald*. Chances were, even if she'd seen it she wouldn't have recognized the name. Only the people who lived close enough to hear his mother screeching at him through the screen door knew Elwood Niedlmeier by his real name.

The constriction eased with a final malevolent ping. Bert glanced at his watch. Two and a half minutes. Not bad. He straightened, waved again, and when Lil's shadow retreated, made one more reckless swoop down the driveway.

Oh, Lil would remember Needles all right. Bert was sure there wasn't a teenage girl in town who hadn't dreamed about cruising the main drag in Niedlmeier's '49 Chevy. The only cruisin' Bert did in high school was on a bike handed down from his older sister, and he sure as hell didn't go anywhere he'd be recognized.

Bert stamped his boots, relieved to feel the thud of concrete through thick rubber soles. No pins and needles. He'd read in yesterday's news about a guy working the stock exchange who complained to the man beside him that his feet were tingling. Dropped dead two minutes later. A young guy. Never got the chance to play Russian roulette with wind-packed snowdrifts and minus thirty. Didn't seem fair with an army of old coots like himself limping around, taking up space.

Bert fished a crumpled handkerchief out of his pocket and blew his nose, keeping his eyes on the Dodge. A plume of exhaust hung on the back like a giant tail feather. Damned cold out here today, but still no excuse for leaving an unlocked car running. Did she think an old fart neighbour shovelling snow was security enough? For all she knew he could be Elwood Niedlmeier. Needles would know what to do if he saw a car purring away with the keys in the ignition. His escapades had landed him in reform school not long after he cracked up the Chevy. From the complicated list of surviving kids in the obit, Bert figured Needles hadn't settled anywhere for very long. No mention of a "loving wife" there either.

Sunlight glinted off the face of Bert's watch. Two more minutes gone, another five before Lil's grey curls would pop out behind the screen door. At least the cold kept her inside. In summer, she parked her lawn chair on the driveway and pretended to read while he circled the square of grass with the mower.

The Caravan was suddenly idling a bit rough. Bert

squinted. The van gleamed, flirting with him against a dazzle of snow and sun. Elwood Niedlmeier, where are you when opportunity knocks? Dead, that's where. Bert wondered if Needles had a warning tingle before The Big One. Hard to imagine a guy like Needles popping nitro.

"Bert?"

Jesus! She'd cut it down to five. Bert put a smooth curve on the bank of snow and hoisted the shovel. A sparkle of ice crystals danced between them.

"Close the door, Lil. You're letting the heat out. If you plug in the kettle, I'll be in for tea in a minute." The door slammed again.

Good old Lil. She'd never leave the car running. Never left the iron on, the water running or went to bed mad. He hated the thought that Lil might look out the window one day and see him toppled like a scarecrow on the driveway. Or turn over in bed one morning and find him stiff and grey beside her on the flowered sheets, mouth hanging wide like a carp.

The door across the street opened and the dippy visitor skipped out, legs flashing in tight green pants. Stan was right behind her. "Hey, Bert!" His voice boomed through the clean air. "You should let me get that for you with the blower." He tapped his head. "Great hat!"

"Don't have to shout, Stan. Sound moves real well through cold air. Even I can hear you."

Stan's guffaw was like the bark of a seal. Always laughing, that guy, like life was a joke. Bert dismissed him with a wave, then turned to hang the shovel in the garage. He gave the sleek fender of the Escort a

28

reassuring pat before he closed the overhead door. His first car was a Ford too. Not in high school, not like Needles. Bert had worked long and hard for everything he owned. Stayed out of trouble, been a model citizen all his life. Look where it got him.

When Bert turned around, the woman had her face pressed to the window, peering into the back of the van. Bert was ready to bet she'd locked the keys inside, but she opened the driver's door, pulled out a big handbag and bedamned if she didn't head back up to the house again.

After the muffled thud of Stan's door there was stillness so pure and clean Bert drank in a lungful of the deadly air just to savour the taste of being alive. He waited, half expecting an angry knee jerk from the angina. Nothing. As sweet a day as you could ask for. Four minutes to Lil.

Funny how clearly he could see Needles' face in front of him after fifty years of hardly giving the guy a thought. Could almost hear that raspy voice. Needles floated there in a puff of exhaust, eyes lit up sneaky and yellow as a ferret's, little smirk that drove the girls wild and the teachers crazy. If it was Needles standing out here in the snow, Bert wondered, would he be dreaming of yanking open a car door, diving behind the wheel, and flooring the gas until all you could see in the rearview mirror was smoke? Due west would be the direction to go. Climbing higher and higher over the Rogers Pass until the big blue sky just reached down and swallowed you up. Yeah, Bert had a hunch that Needles would have hit Revelstoke by supper time.

A playful sunbeam bounced off the door handle.

And then the smirking face in the mist winked. Bert snatched the red toque from his head, crammed it into his pocket, turned up his collar and sprinted to the van. He WAS Needles. Greasy ducktail, pack of Players in his sleeve, split-ass grin and . . . gone!

He slammed the door, yanked off the emergency and, wheels spinning in the packed snow, shot away from the curb. A babble of voices from the radio filled the warm interior of the Dodge. He reached for the dial, killing the CBC. When he hit the highway, he'd find a good country and western station. For now he needed to concentrate, keep well right to avoid the little green Tercel coming toward him. His daughter's Tercel. Bert pulled his head deep into his collar until Deb passed. He checked the rear-view mirror. No brake light. But as his eyes shifted back to the street, his gaze snagged on the smooth plastic curve of a car seat in the back of the van. A seat just like Caleb's. The ears of a knitted bunny cap nodded gently over a sleeping face.

Lord God Almighty! He'd just kidnapped the blonde woman's baby!

Bert cranked a sharp left into the alley. He pulled up out of sight of Lil's kitchen window, and leapt from the van. He bent down, chucked the keys behind the back wheel, and came up facing a pair of saucer eyes. The kid's mouth hung open in that first paralyzed stage of a wail that in ten seconds was going to rival the sirens in the car chase Bert had just imagined for Needles by the time he hit the Coquihalla.

Bert pressed his gloved hand to the window. "Hang in there little fella. She's coming." Then he pounded through the back gate and around the side of the house.

Ramming the Santa cap onto his head, he pulled a ragged breath and strolled into the front yard, chest heaving. In the few seconds it took Deb to lift Caleb out of the car, the door across the street flew open and those green legs flashed in the blinding sun. The woman skidded screaming to the curb, a plastic bag swinging wildly from her arm.

Bert couldn't hear the woman's words past the pounding in his ears. He threw his hands in the air. "Don't worry," he called in the thin tremolo of a harmless old man. "I was just coming to get you. Don't know what went on, but your van's out back here. Baby's fine."

Bert managed a reassuring smile as the woman dropped the bag and flew past on her way to the alley, kicking bright coloured plastic cups across the snow. Now Lil was standing on the step, her cardigan fluttering in the wind, Deb coming toward him, little Caleb holding out his arms to his grandpa.

Bert patted the deep corner of his pocket where the vial of nitro rested. The enemy squeezed harder still.

"Bugger off," he growled in his raspy new voice. "Just bugger off."

THE WAY SHE ATE ORANGES

I grabbed a package of cookies off the grocery shelf, pretended to study the list of ingredients and hid behind my hair. When I peeked out, the woman had pushed her cart into the express line and was thumbing through a tabloid.

Desirée. The name felt as phony on my lips as it had when we were fourteen. I hadn't seen Martha aka Desirée Schmidt since she disappeared in grade eleven, sent to Vancouver to live with an aunt. The last I'd heard, she'd taken a hairdressing course and was working for a mortician. This was from her mother to mine. My mother said she couldn't imagine anyone wanting to share that bit of information.

On the drive home, I convinced myself that I was mistaken. The woman couldn't have been Desirée. For one thing, what on earth would she be doing in Lethbridge? There was just something about her that was unaccountably familiar.

Still, I called my mother, and after catching up on a week's worth of Camrose news, asked, "Mom, do you have any idea where Desirée Schmidt ended up?"

"She's down there in Lethbridge. I told you I saw her mom at Sears about a month ago. Desirée! La-di-da. Still not satisfied with being Martha."

"When did you tell me that? I don't remember talking about Desirée."

"Oh, you do so," she insisted. "You'll probably run into her. Like the women in that old television commercial. You know where the attractive one can't believe how old the other one looks? All because she doesn't use the right skin cream." She paused, sniffed. "The way that girl lived, she'll be the one who needs Pond's."

I hung up the phone, cracked open the package of gingersnaps and ate three of them while I stared out the window into the cotoneaster hedge. While I was trying to invoke the shadowy figures of two little long-ago girls, Jessica came through the door fussing about a costume for the spring concert.

A few minutes later, Emily and three of her friends breezed in. She leaned into the fridge, her jeans straining across her perfect heart-shaped bum, and chucked oranges over her shoulder to the other girls. Emily straightened, and sliced into the peel with her fingernail, and with the first whiff of citrus I remembered as vividly as if she was in my kitchen in ragged jeans, tossing her ironed hair over her shoulder, the way Desirée ate oranges.

I grew up across the street from the Church of God. The manse was one of the oldest houses in town, shaded by Manitoba maples, and with a tiny dormer window above the second floor where I imagined a fairytale bedroom. I'd longed to see the inside of that house for years. When I was eleven, a new minister arrived with a daughter my age, and I finally had the key in my hand.

But I was shy, awkward at making friends. It took a week of my mom's coaxing before I found the courage to knock on the door. The skinny girl who bounced onto the veranda grabbed me by the hand as soon as we'd exchanged names. Martha. She pulled me into a living room that smelled of Lemon Pledge. Silence lay over the house like the lace-edged scarves and crocheted doilies cloaking the furniture. In the kitchen, the scent of Johnson's Paste Wax prevailed and the only sound was the faint buzz of a stern-looking clock over the table.

Martha opened the fridge and threw me an orange. "Let's go outside," she said, "or my mom will make us pray for the hungry kids in Korea."

She zigzagged across the lawn, head thrown back, trying to balance the orange on her chin. Her dad was pushing the lawnmower in slow circles around the yard. His sleeves were rolled to his elbows, but even on Saturday he wore his clerical collar.

"Does your dad always wear that shirt?"

"I think he wears it to bed. His shoes and socks too. Must have taken off his pants a few times though, seeing as there's five of us kids."

I stared at her, at this preacher's daughter with hair so blonde it was white, pulled tight to her skull in a ponytail. A fringe of corn silk bangs clung to her high forehead. Through the fair hair, her skin seemed un-naturally pink and her grey, almost lashless eyes had a feverish look. In three years, she would draw the out-line of her eyes with black liner, let her hair hang from a centre part like limp curtains, and change her name to Desirée. But that day we were still girls, and she grinned and punched my shoulder. "Ha ha. Laugh. It's supposed to be funny."

We sat cross-legged in the tunnel between two rows of caragana separating the manse from the churchyard. "Hey, toss me your orange," Martha said. Unbuttoning her white blouse, she dragged the hem of her undervest free of plaid slacks, shoved both oranges up her front and then stared down in mock alarm. "Oh no! What's happening to my body?"

I giggled, shivered.

She tossed me an orange, warm and slightly moist. I rolled it in the grass before I began to pick at the peel with a blunt nail. She grabbed it back. "Like this," she said, and plunged her thumb into the dimple where the stem had grown. A fountain of juice erupted. She pressed her lips to the orange and sucked, her cheeks drawing in with the effort and her eyes bulging. I reached for the other orange and carefully sliced a cross in the skin with my thumbnail. When I put my lips to the bitter peel they stung. My newly wired braces dug into my lips and I winced. Martha grabbed my chin, peered into my mouth. "I'll never have to wear those," she said. "Vanity is the handmaid of the devil, my dad says. Good thing my buck teeth aren't as bad as my mom's."

We lay on our backs and watched slivers of sunlight

dance in the filigreed branchwork of caragana. By the time Martha finished squeezing and sucking, the orange skin was ragged. She tore it into four sections and pulled away leathery pulp with her fingers. I'd given up after the first few sucks and peeled mine, carefully separating it section by section, and chewing slowly.

"So," Martha said, "who's the cutest boy in grade five?" She licked her palm with lazy strokes of her tongue and I knew without quite knowing why, that I didn't want her to eat an orange when my brothers were around.

The first time she visited our house, Martha wangled an invitation to stay for supper and coaxed my oldest brother into teaching her to "walk the dog" with the yoyo she'd spotted bulging in the back pocket of his jeans. My dad choked on his meatloaf when Martha announced that her mother was going through "the change" and life at the manse was "hell." I'd never heard the word "precocious" until I eavesdropped on my parents' murmurings that night.

"Well," my dad said, "the shoemaker's kids go barefoot and in every brood of preachers' kids there's one little devil."

"Did you see our boys with their tongues hanging out?" my mother asked. "She's ten years old and homely as a mud fence, but she already gives off a scent even tom cats will follow. Thank God we don't have one of those in our family. "

Now, thirty years later, I wondered if Mom realized that God had answered that challenge by giving us Emily. If she'd notice when she came at Easter and took the girls

36

to the mall, how her granddaughter sashayed past teen-age boys, swinging her hips.

The smell of oranges grew even stronger when the girls began lobbing peels at the sink.

With the distractions of supper, and dishes, and homework, I forgot about Desirée until the house was quiet, and Paul and I were propped on our pillows reading in bed. He put his hand on my wrist just as I moved to flip another page. "What, Lainie?"

"What, what?" I shrugged and shook my head.

"You've been sighing every time you turn a page and you're turning them faster than it's humanly possible to read."

I took off my glasses and dropped the book onto the floor without marking my place. "Nothing serious. I saw someone today who reminded me of a girl from home, and she stirred up memories."

"A friend?"

"Long ago," I said, "but I haven't thought about her in years."

That was a lie. When my first husband moved in with my best friend, Jolene, I'd run circles in my head wondering why I'd been stupid enough to hang out with a woman who was the moral clone of my child-hood chum. Larry tried to explain why he was dump-ing me and our two beautiful little girls. "I know I'm a shit for doing this Lainie, but Jolene has something that you wouldn't understand. Other women never do." I understood too well. That certain something had noth-ing do with looks, and it wasn't something you could learn, and it didn't rub off. I knew that from my years of hanging around Desirée, hoping I'd be infected.

37

I did not want to fall asleep with either Desirée or Larry poised to leap into my dreams. I took Paul's book out of his hands and dropped it onto the floor with mine. "Turn out the lamp. I left the blinds open so we could enjoy the full moon."

Long after Paul was asleep, I was still staring at the moon, at the silver-washed bedroom walls. Silver, like my lost charm bracelet.

My grandmother had sent the sparkly chain when I was born, with one tiny sterling silver shoe and the promise of a new charm on every birthday. By the time I was ten, I owned a dangling kitten, ballet slippers, ice skates—a totem for every whim. That first time Martha had come over she'd brazenly poked through the drawers in my bedroom, discovered the bracelet, and gushed over it, begging me to let her wear it. With remarkable gumption, I untwined her spidery fingers and nestled the cluster of silver back into its cotton-lined Birks box.

One Sunday evening a few months later, the charm bracelet disappeared. Right off the top of my pink-skirted vanity table. We were turning the bedroom upside down, my mother and I, when Martha strolled in still dressed in a tartan jumper and starched white blouse. On Sunday she wasn't allowed to change into play clothes or ride her bike, or do anything but read her children's Bible. I was surprised her mom had let her come back after calling her home earlier. Martha sat on my bed, peeled off white cable-knit knee socks and bunched them into her black patent Mary Janes.

"I lost my bracelet," I wailed. "I took it off when I

came home from Sunday school and it's disappeared."
My mother frowned. She had no patience for histrion-
ics and was also less than thrilled that I'd been spending every waking minute, including Sunday morning
at the Church of God, with our boy-crazy neighbour.

Martha sprawled on her back, legs dangling off the
edge of my bed. "You didn't have it on in church," she
said to the ceiling.

"What?" My mother gaped down at her. "I fastened
it for her this morning."

Martha sat up and dug her fingers into her tightly
braided hair, pulling little fans out over her ears so that
she looked like a small animal. She shrugged. "Maybe
she lost it on the way there." Then she turned and stared
at me with those bald grey eyes.

My mom marched us downstairs, out the front door
and back to the church where Reverend Schmidt was
kneeling in silent prayer in front of the cross. He never
looked up, even through Mom's whispered explanation
and our crawling up and down the aisles, peering under pews, shuffling the hymnals in the racks. No sign
of the bracelet in the damp Sunday School room in the
basement, under the wooden steps at the front of the
church or in the lilac bushes bordering the sidewalk.
Gone.

Back home, my mother sat me down on a kitchen
chair. "Was Martha in your room when you took off
your bracelet?"

"No," I said. Hadn't Martha just told us that I wasn't
wearing it in church? And yet I was so sure that I remembered coiling it on the embroidered square of lin-
en that covered my dresser. "Well, maybe . . ."

"I think I'll go over and have a chat with Mrs. Schmidt."

I leapt off the chair and grabbed her arm. "No! Mom, please! Martha would tell me if she knew where it was. She's my best friend." At even the suggestion that she might have done something wrong or told a fib, Mrs. Schmidt would lock Martha in that tiny bedroom until she came out with a confession. Or at least until she'd prayed for about a week. That was how it worked in Martha's house, and this time she'd blame it on me. "She's right. I didn't have it on in church. I must have lost it outside."

The morning after the grocery store glimpse of Desirée, I brooded over a cup of coffee. It was her, Desirée. It couldn't have been. But it had to be. I poured the dregs into the sink and stared at the stain. It was only a matter of time.

A week later at Jessica's concert, the sensation of dropping down an elevator shaft.

"Lainie? I can't believe how lucky this is." Her breathy voice was unmistakable. "My mom called down and gave me your phone number. She ran into your mom or something, but I lost the paper I wrote it on. Or maybe the cat ate it, or maybe my kid." Desirée.

She grinned, showing a crooked eye tooth. "I have a little boy. Imagine. You must have kids too or you wouldn't be here."

I nodded and took the outstretched hand that felt like plasticine. "Jessica's in grade five."

The hair that used to hang like silk drapes frizzled around her face. She looked like she was smiling out of the centre of one of the gerbera daisies the girls always gave me on Mother's Day. A skinny, unremarkable, middle-aged woman. Like Jolene. She craned her neck to look past me at a man two seats away. "Is that your husband?"

I shook my head. I doubted that my mother would have told Mrs. Schmidt that I was divorced, and wild horses couldn't have dragged out of her the details of my living arrangement with Paul. "He's at my older daughter's soccer game. And your husband?"

There was no husband, she told me. Not at the moment. Just her and the little boy in kindergarten. She'd moved to Lethbridge six months ago. I was about to ask why when the lights flickered and a swarm of tissue paper insects rustled onto the stage. She grabbed my arm and pointed to a little bumblebee.

Tulips sprouted and bloomed and eventually, Jessica and thirty-two other grade fives tangled themselves around a wobbly Maypole. But the play was lost on me. I'd fallen back into girlhood, tumbled down the tunnel of green where we ate oranges.

After the finalé, I stood, dazed, and Desirée reached out to hug me, her wrists jingling. She smelled tired, her beige trenchcoat layered with the scents of hair spray, cooking, and a cheap citrusy perfume. When I pulled away, looking first at the gold bangles, then into her eyes, there was no hint of the skinny twelve-year old who'd stolen my bracelet, betrayed my cautious trust.

Two years after my charm bracelet went missing, just after Martha became Desirée, we were crowded into a booth at the Blue Moon Café with a gang of boys who followed her like lost dogs. Her hand darted across the table to snitch one of my French fries and I caught a glint of silver under the cuff of her sweater. Reaching so quickly that I dragged my sleeve through the chips and gravy, I grabbed her wrist and hooked my finger through the chain.

"Where did you get this bracelet?" I shouted. "It's mine. From my Nan!"

She yanked her arm away. "Her Nan," she whined. "Aw, poor baby wants her Nana." The boys laughed and slurped the bottoms of their coke glasses with their straws. Even Tim Kelly, who'd shyly walked me home every day that week. "This is my very own bracelet that my mom and dad gave me, Lainie Irving. You're not the only one who gets pretty presents."

I shoved past Tim's knees and stormed out of the café before I burst into humiliating tears.

I went to school alone the next morning. At the end of the day Desirée walked a block ahead of me, Tim shuffling along at her side.

It took weeks, but finally, without mentioning the bracelet again, we patched up our friendship. Or at least Desirée patched it up enough to borrow my homework when she skipped school and held court at the café. By then, she was hanging out with older guys, and my mother had threatened to tie me to my bed if she caught me in the Blue Moon. Still, whenever Desirée appeared at the back door, I let her in, knowing she'd dance up the stairs, flop onto my bed and spill stories of tongues and hot hands and frantic scrambling for lost panties in the back seats of cars. She was suspended from school twice in grade nine, grounded by her parents so many

42

times she used the dormer window and the trellis at the side of the house more often than the door.

Eventually she teased from me confessions that were more longing than truth, and promised to tell Tim, or Glen, or Curtis that a little bird had whispered that he should call me. She stole the attention of every boy who looked my way. There were only the two after Tim.

I stared now, wondering why she'd turned up again. What was I supposed to learn? Back then I should have learned to watch my back. I'd failed. The point of Jolene, I'd decided just recently, was that she'd speeded Larry's departure and deposited me squarely in Paul's path. The past two years had felt like a chapter borrowed from someone else's life. And now?

Desirée leaned toward me, fingers flicking through my hair, tucking it behind my ear and then pulling one wisp free. "Your hair looks great, Lainie. Have you ever thought about highlights? Where do you get it done? I'm looking for another job."

Did she still, I wondered, work in funeral parlours? Had she ever? So many questions. I tried to avoid looking at the fragile blue-veined wrist, the long cold fingers.

"Let's have coffee," she said. "It's so good to see you." I was embarrassed by the way her eyes shone.

I could see Jessica pushing her way through the bumblebees. "I really have to get home, Martha." Maybe I could put her off for a couple of weeks. I groped for a business card. Maybe she'd lose it, forget about me.

"Oh, that would be great," she gushed, pre-empting my move. "Your place would be even better than a

coffee shop. We don't have a car. And forget Martha."
There was a glint from her eyes like the flash of a blade.
"I'm legally Desirée now. No more Martha."

I flinched. She'd knocked on the screen door, I'd reluctantly held it open and she was pounding up the stairs to my room. Again.

A little boy shoved in front of Jessica and grabbed Desirée's hand. "Let's go. I want a treat. You promised." He had a halo of white-blonde hair.

"We're going to Lainie's house." She knelt in front of him. "We were friends when we were little girls. Isn't that cool?"

He shook his head and the "No" was almost out when Desirée clamped a hand over his mouth. The bottom of his face disappeared, but his eyes had the colour and depth of stainless steel, exactly like his mother's. He stared up at her until she released her palm, then he turned to me and asked, "Do you have Nintendo?"

Desirée planted herself in the front seat when we got to the car, leaving Jessica to glare at me in the rearview mirror. It was rare for Jess to have my undivided attention and I'd promised that after the concert we'd make root beer floats and watch yet another re-run of "Friends." Desirée ignored her as she'd been ignoring her own child since I buckled him into the back of the car.

"What's your little boy's name?" I asked, interrupting a breathless listing of the cities in which Desireé had lived in the last twenty years.

She glanced startled into the back, as though she couldn't remember who was sitting behind us. "Todd." I could feel small shoes kicking the back of my seat.

At first, just an answering tap in response to his name, but accelerating to a maddening staccato. "Stop that, Toddy!" Todd kept kicking until Jessica's arm snaked over to grab his ankle.

In the kitchen, Jessica packed ice cream into two glasses, poured pop into hers and headed for her bedroom, leaving Todd with a can of root beer. I mopped the fizz from the table while Desirée circled the room, lifting and examining everything moveable.

"Jeez, Lainie, you turned into your mom. This kitchen looks exactly like hers. Everything all neat and tidy, a bowl of perfect fruit on the table." She paused beside the sink. "I swear she even had the same little ceramic frog for the dish scrubber."

The ceramic frog was a present from Jessica, just as all the ceramic doo-dahs in my mother's kitchen were Mother's Day gifts. I had no memory of Mrs. Schmidt's kitchen apart from that acrid smell of cleaning products. It was hard to imagine the house where Desirée would live now.

We sat with mugs of coffee and cookies. Todd was installed in front of the television, playing Nintendo. Desirée draped her coat over the back of the chair. She talked non-stop, filling me in on every year of the last twenty. Occasionally she paused for breath and asked, "And what about you, Lainie?" But she never let me squeak out more than a sentence before she was off again.

I began glancing pointedly at the clock. "It must be way past Todd's bedtime," I said.

She looked puzzled for a moment and then laughed. "Oh no, he's a night owl just like me."

Before I could yawn and tell her I was a different sort of bird and had to work in the morning, the back door opened and Emily flew in and sprawled in one of the kitchen chairs.

"We won! We won! And I kicked the winning goal! Can I have coffee?"

And then Paul followed, wearing the blue sweatshirt I loved because it made the streaks in his hair gleam like polished pewter. "Me too!" he said. "A cup of that hot stuff is what we need. It's darned cold out there."

"Martha," I stood up to pour two more cups of coffee, "this is Paul, and my other daughter, Emily. Martha and I were friends when we were kids."

I swear the buttercup yellow sweater Martha was wearing shrank two sizes in the languid stretch that lifted her from the chair to standing next to Paul. She extended that thin white hand, but instead of waiting for a handshake, she rested it on his sleeve. "Gee, Lainie's always had a way of attracting good-looking men." Her smile circled round to include Emily, but when she got to me there was a twitch of irritation. "It's Desirée, not Martha. I'm Desirée Voss. Voss is my first ex's name, but I hung onto it because I like it better than Schmidt or my other ex's name. How stupid is Desirée Drinkle? But Todd, my little boy who's in there playing Nintendo, is Drinkle because otherwise his dad wouldn't pay the child support."

Paul looked bemused, and Emily enthralled. By tomorrow she'd probably have decided that it would be cool to change her name and I was sure "Desirée" would be on the list of possibilities.

I had no intention of refilling Desirée's cup, but she

sat down quickly and held it out. "Your sister looks just like your mom, Emily, but you don't look like her at all. You look like your dad. I look like my dad and I'm really glad because he's a lot better looking than my mother."

Emily's mouth opened, then closed. Reaching across the plate of cookies, she plucked an orange from the bowl of fruit. She knew from my face that an explanation was neither required nor welcome.

Finally, I shooed Emily from the room to finish her homework, and when I left to check that Jessica was getting ready for bed, I found Todd curled up on the floor in front of the television, thumb in his mouth, sound asleep.

"Your little guy needs to be in bed," I said on my way through the kitchen door. "I'll drive you home." Gingersnap in one hand, coffee mug in the other, Desirée was smiling at Paul, at something he'd said. He'd stopped mid-sentence when I walked into the room. Without taking her eyes from his face, she raised the cookie to her lips and licked the sugar crystals from the top with long sweeps of her tongue.

She was quiet on the way home. When we pulled into the parking lot of the condominium complex, she seemed to settle deeper into the seat.

"It's great to see you, Lainie. You were the only real friend I ever had."

She put her hand on my arm. "Let's get together again soon."

When I looked at her face, all I saw was the tip of her tongue protruding from slightly parted lips.

"Martha," I said. "How could we have been such good friends?" My heart was pounding so fiercely, I could feel it in my neck. I raised a hand to hold that pulse in check, as though I was staunching a wound. "You stole from me."

"Oh, Lainie," she said, "it was just a silly bracelet. We were kids. And I gave it back, didn't I? I'm sure I gave it back."

Todd began to whimper then. When I opened my door and lifted him out of the back seat, she had no choice but to get out of the car. He went limp when I tried to stand him beside his mom, and finally she reached down and hauled him onto her shoulder.

"Thanks," she said. "For the coffee and all that." She trailed a finger across Todd's pale cheek. "Can you believe I have a kid?"

I reached out and brushed a hand over his wispy hair. "He's sweet. He looks just like you."

"Everybody tells me that," she said, "but nobody ever met his dad. So how about next week for supper or something?"

I shook my head. "I don't think that will work."

She reached out and clutched my arm. "Oh, I didn't mean to invite myself to your place again." I tried not to wince at the pincer grip of her fingers through my coat. "I'd like to have you guys over—all of you. Maybe Wednesday?"

Todd was waking up, whining and pounding on the back of her shoulders with his fists. I imagined us crowding into her kitchen. Desirée's kitchen. I took a step back, and reached for the handle of the car door. "Thanks, but I'm afraid we're tied up for the next while."

Her eyes narrowed. "You know, Lainie Irving, you haven't changed one bit. You're as spoiled as ever." There was a smell of hot grease in the air. If I'd closed my eyes I would have seen the chalkboard menu on the wall of the New Moon Café. "You don't want to share any of your precious life with me, do you?"

She swirled around with Todd in her arms, her hair electric under the white streetlamp and flew across the parking lot, her coat streaming open behind her.

I sat a long time in the car. A dim light burned over the door through which they'd disappeared. Finally, I started for home.

Paul was still at the table, glasses halfway down his nose, frowning at the sports page. He looked up at me and smiled. "So you revived the childhood friendship?"

I swept the orange peels left at Emily's spot into my hand and carried them across the room to the sink. "More like revisited," I said. When I turned on the garburetor the kitchen filled with the tangy scent of the fruit.

"There's a little coffee left."

I shook my head, but sat down across from him. "I've already had enough to keep me awake." Elbows on the table, chin resting in my hands, I studied the way his hair fell across his forehead, the stubborn cowlick lifting it in an arc over his right eye.

He nipped the corner off the last gingersnap before he handed it to me. "And is she still the same girl you knew way back when?"

I put the whole cookie in my mouth and chewed

slowly. "I think it's more a question of whether I'm the same girl."

"Why don't you invite her for supper some night and find out?"

I reached across the table to brush a crumb from his lips. "No, I don't think so."

"Wait," he said, holding my fingers to his nose. "You smell like oranges."

FROM A STRANGER

When Marcus saw that leather jacket coming toward them with Shane's skinny legs snip-snapping up the path like scissors, he snatched up his baby brother's diaper bag, jammed it into the stroller and grabbed Larissa's hand. But she wouldn't move.

"Come on! Quick, before he sees us." Marcus tugged harder, but Larissa just wiggled the bottle out of Baby Jed's mouth and lifted him onto her shoulder for a burp. Then she pulled out the elastic so that her hair bounced fluffy on her shoulders.

"Too late now, kiddo," she said.

And then, Shane's ugly moustache face was right beside them. "Hey, Mama, you're supposed to leave me a note if you go out. Remember?" His mouth smiled but his eyes were mean. Marcus moved far enough away to be safe from the sweaty, cigarette smell of Shane.

"Aw, Baby, I'm sorry. I had to get outta the apartment. The kids were driving me nuts." She stood tiptoe to put

51

her arms around Shane's neck. Marcus climbed to the top of the slide. He sat with his back to them, hoping nobody else was looking. None of the other moms kissed their boyfriends in the middle of the park.

It didn't last long though. In another minute Larissa and Shane were both screaming. Like always, Larissa was yelling that Shane wasn't her boss, and he couldn't tell her what to do. Except all she ever did was yell about it and Shane just kept right on bossing her. Jed starting bawling in his stroller, and the lady in the blue sweater who always sat on the bench writing got up and moved to another seat beside the lake. The mom of the two boys Marcus had been playing with on the monkey bars hustled them onto their bikes. He was pretty sure they were leaving because of Shane's swears. Someone should have washed Shane's mouth with soap when he was a kid. That's what Marcus's grandma did when he said the soup she made him tasted shitty and he never said "shitty" anymore. Marcus wished he had a bike so he could ride away with those boys.

Instead, he walked toward the lake with his eyes closed, pretending he was blind. When his toes hit the squishy mud, he picked up a rock and hucked it into the water. The geese honked and flapped.

"Marcus! Get outta there. You're gonna wreck your new sneakers."

He ignored Larissa and picked up a smaller stone, clutched it in his fist and waited.

"Listen to your mama, boy. Don't you turn your back." Shane's hand clamped so hard onto his shoulder, Marcus yelped even though he'd promised himself he wouldn't. "I said LISTEN! It's time you learned some respect, little Marcus fart-ass."

"Excuse me?" The voice was friendly but sounded like business, just like Mrs. Franks, Marcus's kindergarten teacher. The lady in the blue sweater held out a plastic bag. "Would your little boy like to feed the ducks?"

Marcus pulled free. The stone he dropped bounced on the toe of Shane's black boot. "Thanks." As soon as he held the bag of grain, the ducks waddled toward him, begging. He was glad his hands were busy so that he could keep from rubbing his shoulder. He was glad Shane didn't tell the lady to eff off. Instead, he'd just given Marcus a shove and went clomping back to Larissa.

The whole day was spoiled now. When Grandma came to take them to McDonald's, and saw Shane's motorcycle out front, she'd leave. He could wait on the sidewalk and ask to go home with her. If he promised to be good and quiet, she might take him this time instead of Jed. "Two little kids is too much," she always said. "The baby's easier." If Grandma took Jed for the night, Shane would talk Larissa into going out after Marcus was asleep. Except he never really fell asleep when he knew he'd be alone.

Marcus shivered. He'd left his batman sweatshirt hanging on the stroller. The bag of grain was almost empty when he noticed one scrawny duck hanging around the edge of the crowd. He tried to shoo the others away but they were mean little buggers. "Buggers" was another word he couldn't say even though his grandma said it. Finally, he gave up trying to throw the kernels over the heads of the big ducks and walked back to the lady to hand her the bag.

She tore the end off a package of gum. The same minty kind his grandma chewed when she was trying to quit smoking. "Would you like a piece?"

Marcus shook his head. Mint things made his throat sting. And boy, would Larissa be mad if she saw him take something from a stranger.

When he started to walk away from the ducks, away from Larissa and Shane, away from the lady, she called to him. "Oh, don't go that way, dear. Your mom won't know where you are."

Mom, Mom, Mom. He never called her Mom. She liked "Larissa" better. Even when she picked him up at school, the other kids called her Larissa.

The lady got up off the bench and stood in front of him, but then squatted so they were eye to eye. They both looked down at the mess of goose poop between them, and then she waddled two steps sideways just like a big old mother goose. Without even thinking, Marcus followed.

She was about to ask him something when Shane's voice and then Larissa's came screeching through the trees.

"How many times do I have to tell you?" Larissa was bawling. "I can't leave him alone anymore. He wakes up, Shane. Last time that snoopy bitch downstairs seen him sitting on the front step at two in the morning."

"I'll talk to him and when I'm done you can be god-damn sure he won't get out of bed until morning."

Even this far away, Marcus could smell Shane. A smell like the stinky dumpster behind their apartment.

The woman flinched. "I'm sure your mom and dad will work it out."

He couldn't drag his eyes away from hers. They were the colour of the lake, right there where the water was shallow and you could see the bottom. Brown, but ripply and green at the same time. No, Larissa and Shane wouldn't work it out. Not ever. They never quit.

But what he wanted most to say was, "He's not my dad." That was the only thing about Shane that made Marcus glad. His dad wasn't a scrawny, mean-face like Shane. His dad was like Marcus. He had blonde hair and big shoulders and in the picture Larissa kept in her underpants drawer, you couldn't see the colour of his eyes because they were all crinkled up in a smile. Sometime Marcus was going to find his dad and tell him about Shane and boy, Shane better look out. The screaming had stopped now. He could still hear their voices but not the words. Larissa was trying hard to talk, but mostly it was Shane.

The lady reached in her pocket and pulled out a roll of Lifesavers. "Do you like butterscotch?"

Butterscotch was his least favourite Lifesaver. It was the only pack left in the little book of candies his grandma gave him for Christmas, but he nodded anyway. She peeled back the waxy paper and he picked the first circle off the roll and popped it in his mouth.

"Your mom's lucky to have a big boy like you to help with the baby."

He stuck his tongue through the hole in the candy to keep it from sliding down his throat. Larissa didn't give him hard candies because he was always choking on things. She'd yelled at Grandma about the Christmas Lifesaver book.

Every adult said the same thing to him about that baby. About how lucky his mom was and how lucky the little pissy baby was to have a brother. Well, he never wanted a brother. And if Larissa just did what Grandma said and gave that baby away when it was born, then maybe old Shane wouldn't be hanging around anymore either.

The pocket of the lady's jacket was dragging, the notebook she'd been writing in about to slip onto the grass, right into the goose poop. Marcus grabbed it before it fell.

Both of their heads jerked toward the flash of denim legs on the path behind the bushes. Shane kicked up a spray of gravel. "Well screw you, Larissa!" he yelled over his shoulder, "Dump that fuckin' kid somewhere and maybe I'll see you later."

Marcus handed the lady her book and looked hard at the ground. He tried to keep his mouth from twisting and he didn't lift his hand to wipe his eyes because she would know then that he was crying. A big tear plopped onto the toe of her clean white running shoe.

"Looking after a baby makes moms and dads cranky sometimes." She whispered even though there was nobody to hear.

"He's not my dad." He wanted the lady to know this. He didn't want her to know the rest but he couldn't keep the words from coming out. "He doesn't mean the baby. He likes that black-haired, squinty-eyed baby 'cause it looks like him."

She looked the way he felt so many times. Like she

was stuck between laughing and bawling. She stood so that she could see over the bushes and Marcus stood too and peeked through the leaves. Larissa was still on the bench, smoking, her back to the lake, to Marcus.

Then the lady snapped open her book and ripped out a page. "Would you like to play a little trick on your mom?"

Marcus shook his head. No way. Larissa didn't like tricks. He didn't like tricks either.

"No," she said, "we shouldn't trick people. But maybe we could teach her something?"

Boy, he didn't know if that would work. It was a long time since Larissa went to school. Grandma yelled about that whenever she was mad at Larissa. About how when she was sixteen years old she had him and she quit school and ruined her life.

"See that clump of trees?"

He followed her pointing finger to some bushes down the path. She scribbled on the torn piece of paper and then handed it to him. "You hide in there until your mom wakes up and looks for you." She pressed the package of Lifesavers into his other hand. "Don't come out until she starts to get really upset. Then tell her this was my idea and give her the note. Okay?"

Marcus chewed on his lip, thinking about what the lady said until he could taste blood mixed with the butterscotch. He looked back at Larissa and even though he couldn't see her face, he knew she was crying about stupid Shane. Then he turned to the brown eyes watching him. The lady didn't look like a stranger. He nodded and shoved the note in his pocket.

Marcus didn't come out when Larissa started to scream, not even when one of the joggers stopped and pulled a cell phone out of his belt and not even when people started running around yelling his name. He stayed there sucking on butterscotch, peeking through the branches. He was down to the last candy when the sirens came. That was when he stepped out of his hiding spot and that was when Larissa grabbed him and started shaking him and he choked on the candy and the policeman had to dig it out of his throat. He couldn't talk, but he pulled the note out of his pocket and handed it to Larissa.

The two policeman looked over her shoulder, and one of them read it out loud. *What's important? Pay attention or someday you'll really lose him.*

The policemen looked at each other.

"Hey! Some goddamn pervert hid my kid in a bush. Aren't you going to find him?"

Marcus told them, when he could finally talk again even though his throat hurt, that it was a lady and not a man and that she looked like his teacher but more like his grandma and then he pointed down the path to show where she'd gone. The policemen looked kind of funny still, but they were watching Larissa, not him. They didn't even think that he might be pointing the other way, not the way the lady went, but the other way.

At home on his bed, Marcus snuffled into Grover's blue

fur and tried to swallow the bad tastes left in his mouth
from choking and crying and too much butterscotch.
Grover was so soggy with tears he looked like he'd been
dragged out of the lake.

The first thing Larissa'd yelled at him when he
stepped out of the bushes was, "I thought you fell in
the lake and drowned!" When she shook him hard by
the neck of his t-shirt, he decided he'd rather drown
than strangle. And right after that, he started to choke
to death on the candy. If Grandma ever got here, he
was going to tell her that Larissa had been trying to kill
him all day. Except it was getting dark now, so Grandma probably wasn't coming.

With a corner of the blanket, he wiped at a snotty
patch on Grover's goofy smile and then pulled the soft
body tight against him.

Marcus was only pretending to sleep when Larissa
came into the bedroom. Her cigarette made a little orange light in front of her face. He tried not to swallow
because his throat hurt and if she heard the gulp she'd
know he was awake and she might yell some more.

Only then, she stamped out her smoke in the ash-
tray in her other hand and sat on the edge of the bed.
He unsquinched his eyes just a little to peek out. Her
face was shiny. The same big moon she'd showed him
last night must be out there, the room was so bright.
Her hair hung straight down her cheeks like curtains,
the way her face was tilted towards him, white as the
moonlight but wet and shimmery like the lake.

"Marcus? You awake?"

She stroked the hair off his forehead and pulled
the blanket up under his chin. Then she dug around

in the pocket of her shorts for a tissue and blew her nose. Marcus turned onto his side with Grover in the crook of his arm. He was so sleepy now, he hoped she wouldn't talk.

When Baby Jed started hollering from the living room, Larissa didn't get up. She sat with Marcus and smoothed the blanket. Her hand came back to rest on his cheek, cooler even than the pillow where he'd turned his face. "Look, Marcus. Don't ever do that again, okay?"

He nodded, too sleepy to tell her he wouldn't.

BIRDWATCHING

Daniel is jubilant. He crashes through the front door, swinging his backpack at the table in an arc that barely misses my binoculars. A mile-wide grin stretches across his small face.

"I got moved. I'm not in Miss Jessop's class anymore!"

My heart pounds out an extra beat of thanks. This morning my tear-streaked nine-year-old pleaded terminal bellyache, drooped beside his school bag at the front door.

"Tell me what happened, chickadee."

Danny grins and flaps his arms. I pour orange juice and sit across the kitchen table while he dumps the jumble from his bag.

"Right after the bell this morning Miss Jessop says, 'Go to the office!' I figured she was mad at me again but when I get there Mr. Thurman just tells me I'm going to Mr. Grey's room 'cause Miss Jessop's class is too big."

He tips his head for the last trickle of juice, mouth open inside the glass. Bright eyes blinking above a Plexiglas beak, he swipes a sweatshirt sleeve across his chin to catch the dribble.

"Then Mr. Thurman says, 'Why don't you phone your mom right now and tell her?'" I said you were out looking for birds and he said to try anyway. But I was right. You weren't here." His smile stretches to two miles.

Ah, Davis Thurman, you coward. While I was scanning the scraggly heights of poplar for my elusive bald eagle, plotting my next visit to your office, you were sweating blood.

Wait another month. That was Mr. Thurman's answer the first time I leaned across his desk and begged. I'd already done my waiting. Sat on my hands and held my tongue for two months. It was now mid-November. Danny's stomach-aches had begun the second week of school. Every day I was tied in sympathetic, gut-wrenching knots by three o'clock, waiting for his dragging feet, his daybook filled with UPPER CASE RED:

DANIEL HAS HAD TROUBLE FOLLOWING INSTRUCTIONS AND ATTENDING TO HIS WORK.

DANIEL'S HOMEWORK IS A MATH EXERCISE THAT THE REST OF THE CLASS COMPLETED TODAY WITHOUT DIFFICULTY.

DANIEL HAS BEEN SULLEN AND UNCOOPERATIVE TODAY.

I used a purple pen scented with violets for my replies:

Daniel responds well to positive reinforcement.

Daniel, as you know, has a learning disability.
Daniel, is VERY VERY unhappy.

Danny chewed his nails to the quick, and the stomach aches got worse. When I took him to the doctor, she sent him to the waiting room while we talked.

"These are symptoms of stress." she said. "What's going on in his life?"

I went to school to find out. While I talked to Miss Jessop, I ran my fingers over the pen-scarred surface of Danny's desk, reading Braille, imagining his body coiled in the seat like a spring that's wound too tight.

"Danny seems to be encountering difficulty, Miss Jessop." If I spoke her language there should be no misunderstanding.

"Mrs. Webber, your son will always encounter difficulty. I do make allowances for his learning disability."

She perched on the desk in front of Danny's, grey wool trouser legs crossed, arms folded in creamy silk. Sleek-feathered goshawk, impassively awaiting my fatal landing.

I searched for calm words until one of her black suede loafers began to tap the floor impatiently.

"Why do you send messages in his daybook that suggest he's lazy?" I asked. "And why does he stay in at recess to finish work that he can't possibly get done in class? That sounds like punishment, not extra allowance."

"The work has to get done somewhere, doesn't it? Daniel's homework is always incomplete."

With tremendous effort I stifled a screech. "Because

he's tired after two hours of homework. Because I let him quit when I know he's past learning. I make the decision, Miss Jessop. I'm the one who should miss recess."

Round and round we flew, my voice climbing, strident. Hers enunciating with exaggerated patience. Any minute, I thought, she would take my face in her hands and look directly into my eyes.

I marched from the classroom to the principal's office.

Davis Thurman is the husband of my old friend, Joyce. Inseparable in high school, in touch through years of moves and changes, Joyce and I have kept a daytime friendship. Our ventures into the evening world as couples have been dismal—Ken thinks Davis is a pompous ass—but Joyce and I still meet for coffee once a month.

In Davis's office, I carefully avoided laying blame on the doorstep of Room Five. But I hinted, just hinted, that Miss Jessop did not seem to understand my son. A personality clash, perhaps.

Davis hitched his words to the tails of mine without even pretending to pause and consider. "You know, Lucy, almost every parent who brings me a problem thinks there's a personality conflict."

Eyes bulging with disbelief, I stared into his unblinking gaze. Great eye contact, Mr. Thurman. Well-honed asset of liars, career-ladder climbers and predatory birds. The carefully preened crest of his hair, glistening eyes, extended neck—pileated woodpecker on the rise. District office before he's forty. I know from Joyce, that's his goal.

"School is a safe environment where children learn to get along with people whose personalities don't always mesh with their own. Teachers have to do it all the time. It's not possible to love every child and it's not likely that your child will love every teacher."

I stretched my neck and all but hissed—Canada goose defending her gosling. "But isn't it the teacher's job to treat every child fairly? To respond to his individual needs? She's not doing that, Davis. Danny is a mess because he hates coming to school. Surely there's a point where it does become a personality conflict? When you can justify moving a child."

He leaned back in his grey tweed chair, fingertips carefully pressed into a tent and regarded me sternly.

"Davis, this is terribly important to me. You know Danny. No wings and halo, not rocket scientist material but with a little help he's going to do just fine. So give him help before all the self-esteem leaks out of him. Please."

The flicker of eyelids, shifting of lines around the mouth, collapse of tented fingers, gave me hope. I pressed on. "Move him to another class. Give whatever reason you want. No other parent will know, I won't tell Danny I came to see you and I will not say another word to Miss Jessop."

"Marilyn Jessop is a good teacher . . ."

I slammed my fist on his desk and kicked the door closed as I stormed out.

I tripled my volunteer time in the classroom. On the third afternoon in two weeks Miss Jessop met me at the door.

"Mrs. Webber. Again? Do you think it's a good idea to encourage this kind of dependence in a nine-year-old?"

Nine years old. Time for a nudge from the nest? On the days I was in the class, Danny glided along with no more than his usual problems with reading. No trips to the office, no red notes in the day book.

"After hanging around that classroom for hours, I have to wonder if he's exaggerating." Ken and I were finishing our coffee while Danny did homework in his room and Travis prowled the kitchen looking for material for a science project—and for tidbits of gossip. At twelve, he is intensely snoopy about adult business. I could almost see his ears tweak in my direction when I started to talk about school.

Ken was oblivious to Travis's eavesdropping. "I suspected that from the beginning," he said. "If she was the witch Danny thinks she is, other parents would have complained and Davis would have gotten rid of her long ago." Ken shook the paper open to the stock market quotes. Done with the discussion.

"Don't close the subject yet," I said. "Maybe she doesn't give him any flack because I'm there. The woman's not stupid."

When I peered at him over the top of his paper he sighed and folded the page.

"Don't you remember teachers who screamed and threw chalk and never heard of self-esteem or positive reinforcement? We survived and so will he. Maybe what she's writing in that bloody journal is true. Danny's decided he doesn't like her and he's not co-operating. He's no angel."

I narrowed my eyes and spoke through gritted teeth. "It's okay for our son to cry every morning because he doesn't want to go to school? You're not here to deal with that. He's no angel, but neither is she the butter-wouldn't-melt-in-her-mouth teacher other parents seem to think she is."

Travis snorted from his station at the kitchen sink. "Teachers are never the way parents think."

"What is she like, Travis? Really. Is Miss Jessop as mean as Danny says?" He shrugged and dumped baking soda into a Tupperware container, vinegar into another. "She always picks on somebody. Last year it was Grady Hoffman."

Grady Hoffman transferred out. To a private school for kids with learning problems. Would that be the answer for Danny? Elfin Danny who bloomed in the gentle sun of three previous teachers. Firm black letters in those daybooks:

DANNY WORKED VERY HARD TODAY.

IF DANNY FINISHES THE MATH HOMEWORK HE WILL BE UP TO DATE WITH THE REST OF THE CLASS.

DANNY WAS A GOOD FRIEND TO NICOLE TODAY WHEN SHE WAS SAD.

I decided to plant a mole. I phoned the class mom again, the one who books the volunteers.

"Lucy, surely you're not looking for more days?"

"No, no. But I might need to trade a day. Tell me who's helping for the next month."

She reeled off a short list of names, all mothers with successful children. They beam and call Miss Jessop "Marilyn". But at the end—bingo. Philomena, my next door neighbour, mother of four scrapping, swearing boys. Philomena said she owned a corner of Davis's office; she said she hated Miss Jessop's frosty beauty, said her Andrew had no problems in the class. Miss Jessop was afraid of Andrew. Philomena would trade days with me and report back with the real goods.

At the end of her volunteer morning, she knocked on my door, empty coffee cup extended.

"Damn right, she picks on him, Luce. But sneaky. Sighs every time he asks a question. Pretends she doesn't see his hand in the air."

She stirred two spoonfuls of sugar into her coffee and raised her eyebrows. Philomena's eyebrows—birds in flight. They give her boys, who have inherited her blue-black starling looks, a hint of devil.

"Get the kid out of her class, Lucy. I'll picket the school with you if that's what it takes."

I shook my head. "I honestly don't know what to do. I've talked to her. I've talked to Davis."

"Davis thinks she walks on water," Philomena said. "They car-pool, for gawd sake. Go back in there and tell him unless he does something you're moving one step up the ladder to the superintendent. Take Ken with you. I always drag Harold along when I need a pit-bull."

I grinned at her. "Philomena, you are an eagle. You soar above the pit bulls. And Ken is neither—he's the voice of reason. He'd come away agreeing with Davis that we just need to give it another month."

But when I tested Ken that night, he surprised me. Ken likes Philomena, trusts her judgment. "Make an appointment for late tomorrow and I'll come with you."

Travis was meticulously slicing cheese and matching each square, corner for corner with a plate of Triscuits. He'd drifted into the room as soon as Ken and I lowered our voices.

He shook his head. "Won't do any good. Mr. Thurman and Miss Jessop are like this." He hooked his index fingers together and reddened as he contemplated the tangle. "I mean, they're always hanging around together. At lunch time they walk to the 7-Eleven to get coffee. Then they sit in the park and talk . . . really close." He waggled his fingers again, this time with a sly hint of a smile.

Ken cleared his throat. "Are you sure about that?"

Travis stuffed a cracker in his mouth and talked around the flying crumbs. "See what I mean? The teacher's always right. All the kids know about Mr. Thurman and Miss Jessop. Me and Craig have seen them down by the river lots of times when we bike there after school."

"Absolutely sure?" I insisted.

He spread his arms, palms up. "Well, maybe not. I never went up and looked in the window. But it's Thurman's car, he's in it and somebody with blonde hair is beside him and they're not watching birds, Mom!"

We sent Travis back to his homework and sat silently, wheels turning. Tumbling in my mind were images of Joyce, smiling at me over a cup of coffee, talking about Davis's plans for the future, their future.

A line of worry rippled Ken's forehead. "Okay. Now we've got the picture. But let's proceed carefully." I think he imagined me storming Davis's office in the morning.

69

"I won't do anything libelous. I'd like to run Davis up the flagpole and leave him there till June if this is why he won't help Danny. I won't even tell you what I'd like to do to him if he's cheating on Joyce. Just imagine a flock of screaming, hungry crows. But give me a day to check this out, and then we'll go see Davis."

I parked in front of the school next day at dismissal, binoculars and camera beside me. When Danny came out and spotted me, I sent him to Philomena's and slid low in my seat, the November issue of MacLean's propped in front of my face on the steering wheel. I wished I had a minivan like the six others parked around me. My red Honda glowed like a stop light. When the vans pulled out, I backed halfway up the block until I could just see the staff entrance.

Slowly the teachers' parking lot emptied, until only the caretaker's truck and Davis's ancient Volvo remained. The car, Joyce often said, that was more beloved than she and the kids. Finally Davis emerged, dressed in a natty camel coloured overcoat, briefcase in one hand, gently guiding Marilyn Jessop's black wool-clad elbow with the other. He opened the passenger door for her and while he stowed his bag in the back seat, I eased off the emergency brake and crept to the corner. I lurked a block behind until we were out of the neighbourhood, and put two cars between us as we merged onto the freeway. So sure now of where we were heading, I signaled at the exit before Davis did and dropped back as the traffic became lighter on the road into the park. Four o'clock on a November afternoon is not a busy time at the riverside picnic area.

70

Davis turned into a parking spot facing the water. Surely they could have found a cosier rendezvous. The river rippled by, gulls swooping between scummy clouds and grim pewter waves.

As I passed Davis's car, I hunched into the hood of my coat. Providence had placed a gigantic garbage bin at the next picnic site. I glided in on crunching gravel, stepped out of the car, and from behind the bin, focused my binoculars on the driver's window of the Volvo.

Done with talking, Thurman and Jessop had merged into a tangle of hair and sleeves.

I crept from tree trunk to tree trunk, glad that I had impulsively grabbed Travis's grey parka instead of my own emerald green coat. I resisted the temptation to dart. That much I knew about stealth. When I was finally close enough to see, the side windows gave zero visibility. Steamed up.

I flipped the binoculars over my shoulder to dangle on my back, queasy at the thought of a close-up. Caught a flicker of Davis's eyelids as I passed in front of the car.

Marilyn Jessop raised her smudged face just as I clicked the shutter, lifted a hand in farewell and loped back to the car.

Danny puts his glass in the sink, shines an apple on the thigh of his blue jeans and skips downstairs for an hour of television before supper. I wipe up the drips of juice on the table and retrieve my photo order from my purse. Downy woodpecker, snowy owl, bald eagle and a magnificent gathering of magpies are all in perfect focus. The last picture is fuzzy but there is no mistaking the stricken faces.

When Ken comes in, I hand him the photo.

"Whoa!" He flings it onto the table. "Lucy . . . "

"Relax, "I say. "It's already done the job." Then I tear the picture into tiny pieces and bury them deep in the kitchen garbage.

POCKETS

Mary Jo is not allowed to shop. Not in person. Her twin sister, Patti Sue, who says she'll move to Nunavut if she's called to bail out Mary Jo one more time, imposed the shopping ban.

"Emjay," she said a year ago, "technology is going to save you. You can order everything from kiwi fruit to tampons on-line."

Indeed, technology did keep Mary Jo's life under control until today, when she came home from a late afternoon run and found Troy in bed, the quilt pulled tight under his chattering jaw.

"The doctor thinks I have strep throat," he croaked. "There's a prescription in my jacket pocket."

Instinctively, Mary Jo stepped back, rubbing her hands on her thighs, wishing the slick fabric of her running shorts could whisk away the expectation that hung between them in the dim bedroom.

They've lived together for only one month. Before

Troy moved in, Mary Jo held a lungful of breath while she showed him the internet bookmarks for online shopping, the Rubbermaid bins that are set out in the hall on Friday morning for the Organic Harvest delivery. The inventory of toilet paper, Kleenex and stationery on the top shelves of the linen cupboard. She waited for a reaction—a shiver of incredulity, the uneasy laugh—waited to breathe. He wrapped his arms around her, and held her tight. Eyes closed, willing fabric and flesh to melt, Mary Jo imagined herself so fused to Troy's lean body that her own shape was nothing more than the shadow of a spine, a trilobite.

"You mean you won't drag me through stores?" he asked. "No supermarkets, antique shops, gift emporiums?"

She exhaled, flicking her tongue into the warm hollow of his throat like a lizard drunk on dew. "No, we have more important things to do with our time."

Mary Jo wishes she'd run this morning instead of waiting for the rain to stop. If she'd been home when Troy stumbled in, there would have been options. She is quick. Even when she's caught off-guard, she draws from a bag of tricks. Sleight of hand. Sometimes she pulls it off.

She works at home. This too simplifies her life. Her mother says her gift for languages really is a gift—God trying to make up for "the other." With an M.A. in Romance languages and a reputation as a perfectionist, she's able to earn a decent living as a translator. Today, she's been working on a Portuguese cookbook. Midway through the morning, the recipe for *Empanada de Galinha* set her mouth watering. She stopped work and began to cook. When the chicken was browned and simmering in wine, the bread dough rising, she tied on her shoes and set out for a five kilometre run. By the time she got back, there was this problem of picking up Troy's medicine.

Mary Jo could phone a drugstore in Quebec, or even Madrid for that matter, and make herself understood, but there isn't a single pharmacist in this city who can comprehend that she needs to have Troy's prescription delivered. They tell her that legally they must have either the written script in their hand or the authorization of the doctor by phone. The doctor's office is closed.

She stalls, opening a can of chicken broth and ringing her sister and her mother while it heats. No answer. Mary Jo can't believe that Patti Sue is "unavailable" to take her call. Their mother is at bingo, says the permanent message on her answering machine. She's been at bingo during every crisis Mary Jo can remember. Maybe it's just as well.

She pours the soup into a ceramic bowl the color of opal, sets it on a napkin-draped tray, adds four soda crackers and a glass of ice water. The soup is a perfect golden pond with a curl of steam rising like morning mist.

Unfortunately, Troy is too sick to appreciate the artistry. His eyes are closed and his jaw slack. The air in the room is hot and moist. It smells like the dishwasher in mid-cycle. Mary Jo leans over the bed, pulls the blanket ever so gently up to his chin. "Sleep tight, sweetheart," she murmurs. "We'll get that medicine first thing tomorrow." And then she turns to tiptoe out of the room.

"What?" Troy heaves himself up on his elbows.

She inches toward the door. "Try a few sips of broth. It'll shrink your mucous membranes and you'll be able to fall asleep. You'll feel so much better by morning."

He groans and drops back onto the pillows. "Please, Mary Jo. If you don't go to the drugstore tonight, I'll have to do it myself."

"If you can get up, how about a bath? The steam will help your chest. While you're in the tub I'll get on the Internet and find some good natural remedies."

"I'm an economist!" His voice is strong for someone so stricken. "I'm not interested in cures involving rhubarb." He grabs a fistful of tissues from the box beside the bed and blows his nose. "The prescription," he says, "is in my jacket pocket. Please."

She finds Troy's jacket on the floor in the living room. Why didn't he just stop and pick up the medication himself? Because he was sure he could count on her. In the three months since they met, there have been no denials, no doubts, no disappointments.

Eyes closed, she visualizes stepping through the automatic door into the ugly white light of the drugstore. She will walk to the back of the store, hand the pharmacist the prescription, watch him count tablets, slide them into a bottle. Then she'll pay, turn around, and leave the store. She takes a deep breath, her heart pumps quietly. She can do this.

Mary Jo plucks a blue raincoat from the closet. Her hands glide through the silky lining of the sleeves and into the pockets as easily as fish through a cool stream. The coat is as blue as the last hint of dusk in a winter sky. A color she seldom wears, preferring shades of green that ignite the sparks in her Titian hair. Head cranked over her shoulder, she tugs the collar away from her neck and squints at the label. London Fog. This is a fine coat.

She slips the prescription and her wallet into the deep pocket of the coat before she steps into the October evening. Two blocks from home, she passes the neighborhood pharmacy tucked into a strip mall between the bakery and pizza parlor. Well over a year since she's been in that store, but the same man has counted pills from the dispensary at the back as long as she can remember. And his wife at the front, selling Lotto 649, watches over the cash and the short aisles of the store like a hawk. Mary Jo remembers the hard coral line of the woman's lips. She remembers the woman's nails like claws on her wrist, dragging her hand from her pocket. She hates the store. And so she zigzags down quiet residential streets for at least two kilometres, her heels splashing an icy spray that raises goosebumps on her bare ankles.

The rain has stopped but the sky is so overcast she feels as if the clouds are riding on her shoulders. At another, larger strip mall she pauses in front of the Wild Bird store. A squirrel-proof bird feeder in the window is the same as one she bought for her mom two birthdays ago, before cyber shopping.

Inside London Drugs, she makes a beeline for the dispensary, stands in front of the drop-off desk drumming an agitated beat with her fingers while the pharmacist hands a small white bag to a woman whose cheeks are flushed in perfect scarlet circles. Mary Jo, hands pressed to the counter, stares at a cabinet-banked wall in the dispensary.

Finally the man takes her slip of paper. "It'll be about twenty minutes." His voice is tired.

Mary Jo can feel the cavernous store at her back and imagines a cold wind rushing toward her. Twenty minutes. She licks her lips. "It's an emergency," she says quietly. "My boyfriend is very sick. Don't you have some kind of priority system? Like triage?" Someone behind her sniffs.

The pharmacist glances at the prescription, then rubs his eyes. "This is an antibiotic. It won't make a difference for at least forty-eight hours so really twenty minutes . . . ." He sighs. "What do you have for relieving the symptoms meanwhile?"

During the dialogue that follows, Mary Jo is aware of muttering, of hostile tension bonding the waiting customers. Without looking behind her, she moves to the cold preparations. She is never sick and has no idea what Troy has added to the medicine cabinet. Although he has a plethora of bottles on top of the fridge and gulps down vitamins every morning with his orange juice, she doesn't remember seeing decongestants. It won't hurt to follow the pharmacist's advice. The words "comfort," "relief," "sleep," resonate. Yes, this is what she wants for Troy. For both of them.

The queue is even longer when she stacks her selection of cold remedies on the edge of the counter. She shoves her fists into her pockets and turns her eyes to the ceiling. The store is too hot. The air smells like open jars of Vaseline and dust and stale packaged cookies.

The lights cast a ghoulish green complexion on the

faces staring numbly at rows of vitamins. Mary Jo's toes curl inside her black loafers and the tension begins to travel. The backs of her knees tighten. She shrugs her shoulders, rolling her head to relax her neck. A display in front of her holds travel-sized containers of shampoo, conditioner, hair gel. Bins and bins of tubes as bright as candy.

She hears Patti Sue's voice in her head. Get out. Get out. Get out!

Mary Jo drifts down the aisles. Past Tampax, hair color, toothpaste, into the cosy corner of cosmetics, along the jumble of sale items at the front of the store. She peers at toasters and deep fryers, mops and brooms, dinner sets. From Stationery she can see two clerks chatting in the computer department, their eyes on a customer rifling through a display of ink cartridges.

Last week Troy made a late night run to this very store for a new printer cartridge so that she could meet a morning deadline on a set of Italian documents. She can count on Troy. And Troy is counting on her. Mary Jo feels a ping in the back of her skull, like an elastic pulling her back to the dispensary.

The pharmacist looks up, smiles as though as he's been waiting all evening for the pleasure of her visit, and carries Troy's pills to the cash register. Now the store seems almost empty and Mary Jo imagines the man closing cabinets and locking the till as soon as she's signed the credit card receipt and tucked the bag into her pocket. She's four steps away when his voice drops over her like a lasso. "Just a minute, please."

Mary Jo stops, both feet glued to the white tile, and fumbles for the best trick in her bag. But she's already spoken in perfect English. It's too late to stare blankly and pour out a torrent of Spanish. She turns slowly.

Surprisingly, the man is smiling. "Did you want these other things you left on the counter?"

Mary Jo smiles back. Her heart hammers against her breastbone. She shakes her head. "No. I don't think so."

The trip to the front of the store is like walking barefoot in sand. Outside the door, she fills her lungs and the night is like champagne bubbles in her chest. The ceiling of cloud has lifted leaving a purple arc underlit with gold in the west. She feels inches taller, and indulges in a saucy pirouette in front of the window of the bird store. Her hair caresses the silky blue shoulders, and she looks fresh-faced, purposeful, in her nicely cut raincoat. Yes, she sees the image of a young woman with somewhere to go.

On the other side of the street, a car lurches to a halt, tires scraping the curb. Mary Jo's fists clench. Her sister pounds across the parking lot. "Emjay!" Breathless in front of Mary Jo, Patti-Sue grabs her arms. "Ohmigod, I phoned when I saw your number on the call display and Troy said he thought he was dying and he sent you to the store. He didn't know exactly where you were going and I've been to three other drugstores already and I was worried sick." She exhales. "Are you okay?"

"Troy's the one who's sick."

"You know what I mean." Patti's face is so close her breath leaves a little cloud between them. Mary Jo pulls away.

Looking into her sister's face is like looking into the wavery glass of an old mirror. One eye is slightly lower, larger than the other. The mouth pulls toward the right ear on one side, tugs down to the jaw on the left. The hair is heavy like Mary Jo's, but without lustre. Although she is only twenty-eight, tiny fans radiate from Patti's eyes and the corners of her mouth, the skin along her jaw showing a tendency to sag, to crackle like peeling silver. She could do so much more with herself. Mary Jo should take her back into the drugstore and march her to the cosmetic counter. But the last thing she wants is to spend time with Patti Sue when Troy is waiting for her. Now that she has the prescription, she doesn't need help. She pulls the belt of her coat tight, and crosses her arms over her chest.

"I was feeling so good because I managed this little mission, and here you are streaking through the night to save me. Why? Won't you ever trust me, Patti?"

Her sister flinches as though she's been slapped. "I'm sorry." She's dumpy in jeans and sweat-shirt. Exactly the same height as Mary Jo and the same weight, but Patti has always looked as though a fall from a great height has destroyed the springs in her body. Poor Patti Sue. She needs to get a life. To quit riding on Mary Jo's coattails. But Mary Jo feels a twinge of guilt for all the times Patti Sue has come to her rescue. Since she met Troy, she hasn't made time for anyone else, and especially not her sister.

Arm around Patti's shoulders, she turns the two of them to face the window. "How about driving me home?" She flicks out her tongue at the reflection. "Mary Jo and Patti Sue. If Mom had a couple more daughters we'd be a hillbilly band."

Finally Patti sighs and relaxes under Mary Jo's em-

81

brace. "Mom used to say she should have stopped at plain old Mary so that nobody would recognize your name in the papers when you got in trouble."

What Mary Jo remembers is her mother screaming at her when she was sixteen. "Why couldn't I have had just one baby? Poor Patti Sue! They wouldn't let her into the drugstore today because they thought she was you!"

Still linked, they walk across the road to the car. On the short drive, Mary Jo leans back and closes her eyes. If Patti Sue would just shut up, the lovely giddy feeling might return, but she babbles on.

"I found a fantastic on-line shoe store. You can print outlines in different sizes and then fold them to make a paper shoe so you can see how they'll actually look on your foot. They guarantee a perfect fit. I'll show you."

"Stop." Mary Jo's voice is metallic, like a spoon ringing against the inside of a tin cup.

"What?" The car slows to a crawl next to the curb.

"Not the car! I mean stop finding things for me. Stop organizing my life."

Patti's foot lands heavy on the gas now, her eyes straight ahead on the long stretch of wet pavement, and they speed down the last three blocks. "I'm trying to help you."

"You can quit. I'm fine."

She signals, turns, slows as she approaches the apartment building. "Are you sure about that?"

Mary Jo gathers herself inside the blue coat and pulls into the corner of her seat, her shoulder to the door, her body turned so that she's facing her sister. "Three

82

months ago you promised that you and Mom would both get off my case. Isn't it about time?"

"Emjay, you've practically been under house arrest. How can you know?"

"I went to the dentist last week, for God's sake!" Mary Jo fingers the lapel of her raincoat. Just inside the door to the waiting room there was a coat tree. "I was fine."

"A dental office is not a store." They've pulled into the parking lot at the side of the building. Patti Sue takes her hands off the steering wheel and faces Mary Jo. "You heard from Mom? I've been trying to get hold of her all week, but she's never home."

"No." Mary Jo sighs, feeling sorry again for Patti who spends her life keeping track of her twin and her mom. "But whenever I do, it's worse than the Spanish Inquisition." She mimics her mother's scratchy, cigarette voice. "What do you mean there's a man in your life? How many times do you have to get dumped? There's nobody gonna put up with your shenanigans and the sooner you accept that, the better."

Patti Sue's face softens. "I think she's wrong. He's a sweetheart, Emjay, and it's obvious that he's nuts about you. You're sure it'll work?"

Mary Jo puts her head back and smiles through the windshield at a velvety sky. "Everything is wonderful." But she sits up abruptly when Patti Sue takes the key from the ignition and opens her door. Mary Jo grabs her arm. "You can't come in. Troy's so sick it's disgusting. The place is crawling with his virus." When she looks up at their apartment the only light is the stunning reflection of a gibbous moon in the bedroom win-

83

dow. "I'm going to creep around like a little mouse so I don't wake him up."

Patti Sue slowly swings her legs back into the car. "Okay." She seems to be chewing on a thought, her teeth working her bottom lip. "Emjay, I get the feeling you don't want me to be around Troy. You've been going out with the guy for ages, living with him for more than a month and I've only met him once."

Mary Jo puts her hands on her sister's hunched shoulders and leans toward her. "We've just been so busy." Cheek pressed to Patti Sue's, she sighs. "I know I've kept him to myself but I have to make this work, Patti."

A cloud wisps across the moon and she imagines Troy turning his face to the window. "I'd better go. He's going to wonder what's happened to me."

"I can't believe he sent you to a store." Patti's eyes narrow, watching like a cat. "Emjay, exactly how much does Troy know about you?"

Mary Jo shrugs and slides out of the car. "Everything he needs to know. Thanks for the lift. I'll call you tomorrow." As she runs to the building, the frosty grass crackles under her feet. Behind her, Patti Sue is calling, but Mary Jo only turns once she's inside the double doors. Her sister's mouth opens and closes and she tugs at the sleeve of her sweatshirt. Mary Jo shrugs, fits her key in the lock pretending that she doesn't understand the pantomime, can't read lips. But she wonders why it's taken so long for Patti to shout, "That's not your coat!"

Vial of tablets in one hand, glass of water in the other, Mary Jo tiptoes into the moonlit bedroom and sits at the foot of the bed watching the laboured rise and fall of the blanket. When Troy stirs she slides closer, sets the glass on the bedside table and strokes his forehead. His skin feels slick and hot under her fingertips. Her hand shakes, barely able to handle the childproof lid. When Troy reaches for the light, she catches his wrist. "No, don't. It'll hurt your eyes. Here." She slides a capsule between his dry lips, and he drains the water and then kisses her palm. Eyes closed, Mary Jo fights to keep her hand from scrubbing itself on the sheet.

"You'd better sleep on the couch," Troy says. "Do we have anything that'll help me breathe?"

While she's on her way to the bathroom to look, Mary Jo slips her hand into her pocket and feels a flat cardboard shape. Frowning, she holds a box of Dimetapp up to the light. Now why did she let that pharmacist talk her into buying these after all? The other hand plunges deep into the second pocket and she laughs out loud. Crayons? Dentucreme? He's given her someone else's things as well.

On the way back to the bedroom she tries to replay the evening in her mind, fitting segments together like bent and peeling jigsaw pieces. Troy is sitting up now, his back against the headboard of the bed. He pats the sheet beside him, and takes the Dimetapp from her hand.

"Thank you. You really do hate stores, don't you?"

"The pharmacist said it'll be forty-eight hours before the pills take effect."

The moon bathes Troy's face in silver. He shimmers in front of her, like a mirage that will disappear if she comes too close. But when he cups her cheek in his hand, she leans into him. His lips quiver in her hair, she feels his breath hot on her ear. "I was worried," he whispers. "Patti Sue phoned and went ballistic when I told her where you were."

Mary Jo feels cold fingers around her heart. She shivers. "Patti Sue has some problems, Troy. Some very serious problems."

Now Troy's hand is warm on her back. He strokes the smooth blue fabric and straightens her collar. "Where'd this come from? Another on-line order?"

Mary Jo feels as though she's drowning in moonlight. She closes her eyes. With her face against Troy she smells the heat of his body, tinged with a faint scent of unfamiliar perfume from the folds of the coat.

STITCHES

There is a knot in the thread. So close to the end of the hem, the woman pauses to tug each stitch through the fine cloth.

These are her mother's hands, her grandmother's hands. Always stitching. Christening gown, plaid jumper for first day of school, red velvet Christmas frock, graduation dress, wedding gown, christening gown. Sewing the lives of daughters.

The girl on the floor squares her shoulders, braces palms on either side of blue-jeaned legs and drinks a deep breath. "I have to tell you something," she says on the exhalation.

The fabric puckers. "I wish I had a finer needle, and lighter thread," the woman says. "I wish you'd asked me to do this when I got here yesterday instead of when I'm halfway out the door."

"Mom! Will you just listen?"

The daughter's voice stumbles over words. The

mother's vision blurs. She crosses her knees to bring the work closer, head bent to the needle. Measures her stitches smaller, tighter.

She wants to cover the soft lips with her palm, to say *No telling is needed. While you were at your class this morning I did what visiting mothers do. I tidied and snooped.* But it seems she's sewn her tongue to the roof of her mouth.

A photo frame lay flat, folded, face down. It's usual position, upright, drawn in clean lines on the dusty desk top. She'd picked it up and tilted the glass to the sweep of window in this twenty-second floor student apartment, sunlight turning the faces in the picture to spangles.

A triptych of two girls. No. Two women. In the first frame both squint solemnly into the distance, in the second they smile their secret to the camera, and in the third unabashedly into one another's eyes. Telling this mother what she already knew.

The girl is still again. So quiet the room, the sound of the last stitch piercing the cool skin of fabric is audible.

How to keep the wrong words from exploding. Bouncing off the wall of light and ricocheting around the room.

How to say *thank you for telling me.*

When she stands to gather her girl into her arms, the dress refuses to slide free, dances instead from where she's stitched it to her lap.

In a minute she will pick up the scissors. Snip her daughter free. Stitch by stitch.

LEFTOVERS

Before she died, Margaret Murray cooked, packaged, labelled, and froze enough food to nourish her husband for a whole year. She also planned her funeral and gave away her clothes, but it was the meals that astonished anyone who heard the story. "Who could eat that food?" they inevitably asked. Frank Murray just shrugged. To ignore or dispose of the frozen labour of love would be to turn his back on Margaret, and he had decided twenty years before that he would never do that again.

Margaret's grandmother, mother, and sister all died of breast cancer, and she had fatalistically announced at her sister's funeral that she too would die before her fifty-fifth birthday. Pessimism typical of a Capricorn, her friend Sandra had said. Margaret was fast approaching fifty-four.

On the December day that Margaret heard the results of the critical mammogram, Frank was so sure all would be well that he stopped to buy chocolates on his way home from work. Four hand-dipped Belgian truffles in a gold foil box.

He expected, as he came through the door, to hear Margaret call out as usual from the kitchen, "In here, Frank! Supper in half an hour." She was sitting in the living room in her wicker rocking chair. When he took the cup from her slack fingers, cold tea sloshed over the rim and across his knuckles. He reached toward the lamp but Margaret grabbed his hand, her face a solemn white moon.

"There is a lump." She stared down at the front of her sweater. "How can it be that we didn't feel it? Neither of us. I was so sure I'd find the lump myself. I thought I'd worry over it and feel it there and then gone and then back again for at least a week before I made an appointment. That's how I thought it would be." She stood up, grabbed his hand and slid it under her sweater, peeling away the cup of her bra so that the weight of her breast rested in his palm. She pressed his middle finger into soft flesh. "There," she said. "Right there about four o'clock from the nipple, is what the x-ray showed. Can you feel it?"

Her skin was reassuringly warm and pliant. Frank shook his head. "No," he said. He wanted to pull his hand away, but to do so he would have to wrench free of Margaret. And now, even though he didn't feel a lump, there was something. A needle of heat radiating from deep inside his wife's breast.

"I have an appointment with the surgeon," she said. "Next week. How's that for service in a backed-up medical system?"

90

He gently withdrew his hand. "No," he said again. "I can't feel it." But the sensation, like the sting of a wasp, stayed on the tip of his finger. "What will happen at that appointment?"

"A biopsy," she said. "But that's it, Frank. I'm not going any farther than the biopsy."

When Margaret's sister was reduced to a bald shadow of herself, Margaret had wiped away tears after their last visit to the hospice and announced that she would have no part in such a drama. No radiology, no chemo, no frantic searches for alternative medicines. The ending was written, and Frank knew that no amount of discussion would convince Margaret to change her mind. She went into the kitchen, slammed a skillet onto the stove and made scrambled eggs and toast for their dinner.

Later, Margaret curled up in her rocking chair in a fuzzy blanket, sifting through recipe cards, making the four chocolates last by nibbling rodent-like around the edges, licking the ooze of the soft centres from her fingers. Normally, this would have driven him crazy, driven him downstairs to putter in his workshop, but he stayed, and made a pot of tea, and brought Margaret's cup to her with a wet napkin.

Outside, the wind tore at the corners of the house and piled icy drifts against the doors.

On a December evening a year later, Frank and his two children said goodbye to the last of the funeral guests, and drifted single file into the living room.

Michael sprawled on the couch. "Weird music, huh? I mean the hymns didn't surprise me, but what was that last song? The one for us."

Hands in his pockets, Frank stared out the living room window. The weather was uncommonly mild, the pavement shining black under the streetlights. At the cemetery the upright stones in the old section had caps of melting snow like dripping ice cream cones.

"Forever Young." Neither the request of that song, nor the fact that it was dedicated to her children had surprised Frank when he opened the envelope with Margaret's carefully drawn funeral plans. *And don't,* she'd written, *ask your cousin Marlene to sing. Someone's sure to suggest her. Just play the CD. The church organist will do just fine with the other two songs.* The only problem had been in finding the CD. Andrea claimed it had a permanent place on top of the fridge with the player, but there was no trace when she and Frank searched the house. Finally, she'd downloaded the song from the internet, ignoring Frank's concern that this was theft, something Margaret wouldn't have approved of.

"May you grow up to be righteous . . . " the song ran. But he didn't point that out to Andrea.

Frank didn't know the other two songs, hadn't attended church with Margaret, but from the swell of harmony in the rows of Margaret's family, he guessed they were familiar hymns. Beside him, Andrea had joined in on the chorus of the first one, then stopped with a heart-wrenching gulp.

"You don't remember the song? Where did you grow up?" Andrea walked around the room gathering napkins and cups. Frank was surprised Sandra hadn't insisted on staying to help with the clean-up. "It's from that Joan Baez tape she played until it wore out and we replaced it with a CD last Mother's Day. What on

earth are we going to do with all the leftover food?"
She nudged Michael's foot with her toe. "Help me haul
some of those cakes and squares downstairs."

Frank followed them to the kitchen, blinking in as-
tonishment at the tower of Tupperware on the table.
Arms loaded, they carried the baked offerings to the
freezer. The cavernous chest was full. "You won't have
to worry about cooking," Margaret had told Frank
months ago. "There's a year's worth of meals in the
freezer." He'd thought she was exaggerating.

"What is all this?" Andrea lifted a package from the
right-hand side of the freezer, read the label. "*171.
Meatballs in mushroom sauce. Thaw and heat in microwave. Serve with rice and please eat salad every day.*
Dad?"

"Your mom did some cooking before she got really
sick." There'd been days last winter when the windows
dripped steam from the bubbling pots, and Margaret's
hair, when he buried his face in her neck, smelled so
strongly of onions and meat that it made him gag.

"And you're going to eat this stuff! How could she
do this?" Andrea slammed down the lid of the freezer.
"And the other thing I'll never understand is why she
decided to just lie down and die without even trying.
As though it didn't matter." She began to pile the baking on top of the clothes dryer. There was a yellowed
sheet of instructions taped to the control panel, relic of
the first time Frank and Margaret had gone on vacation
alone and left two teenagers behind. The enormous
freezer dated back even further. Margaret was a frugal,
well-organized woman, buying in bulk, always cooking
for tomorrow as well as today.

Frank opened the freezer once more, and began wedging plastic containers into the deep crevice between the baskets that divided the freezer in two. When his hands were free, he stood behind his daughter and rested them on her shoulders. "Andy, the doctor said it wouldn't have mattered. This cancer was so aggressive and so advanced . . . "

Andrea turned on him, nose to nose. "It did so matter!" she shouted. "If she'd told me how bad it was, I could at least have come home in time to say goodbye!" Then she ripped the paper off the dryer and crumpled it into her pocket before she ran up the stairs.

Andrea wandered down the street to Sandra's house the next morning looking for the kind of comfort, Frank thought, that her mother had always provided. Sandra had been the only other young mom on the block when Frank and Margaret bought their house twenty-three years ago. Sandra's husband had once told Frank that the labour unions he negotiated for looked pale beside the formidable friendship of their wives. Over the long months of illness, Frank had marvelled at Sandra's buoyancy to the point of wondering if she didn't know her best friend was dying. The night he knocked on her door to tell her Margaret was gone, she'd refused the arms he'd hesitantly held open, tears flying off her cheeks when she shook her head and he'd left, relieved that she'd chosen a private grief. The next day Andrea arrived home from Montreal, and Sandra was at the door, clear-eyed and as warm and comforting as the plate of cinnamon buns in her hand.

About noon, Andrea and Sandra appeared with the

intention, they said, of putting the house in order. A strange euphemism, Frank thought, for getting rid of Margaret's belongings. Sandra knew that the house was in good order. Although Margaret had railed against it, they'd had a cleaning lady for the last six months. After years of Margaret's slap-dash housekeeping, Frank had found comfort in the tidy rooms. Margaret had turned her small remaining energy to making lists. While Andrea and Sandra walked silently down the hall to the bedroom, Frank pulled out a file folder—the only thing left in Margaret's desk—and re-read the note.

There are books and CD's and a few other things for Sandra in the small grey Samsonite, but tell her to please return the suitcase. It's the right size for carry-on, for when you go to visit Andrea. My jewellery's in the big bag with some other treasures for Andrea (except for your mother's ring in the safety deposit box. She wanted one of Michael's children to have that someday—do you think that will ever happen?) Let Andrea keep that suitcase because I don't imagine you'll be going on any long trips. You never did like travelling.

He was on his way to the basement to retrieve the bags when Andrea called to him. In the bedroom, Frank found the two women looking bemused. "It's done. There's nothing here," Sandra said, waving her hand toward the open closet. All that was left was a new nightgown that Sandra had brought to cheer Margaret up just a week before she died and the outfit Margaret had worn for her visits to the doctor. In the last months the grey wool slacks and red sweater had hung as life-lessly on Margaret's jutting bones as they did in the bare closet. Hangers jangled when Andrea removed the small cluster of garments.

Frank shook his head. Two days before, he'd been blind to the empty hangers when he lifted out a dove-grey dress to deliver to the funeral home. There'd been no major purge of closets and drawers that he could re-member, but a steady trickle of green bags for Frank to haul off to the Salvation Army bin. He found it odd that Margaret hadn't told Sandra about the housecleaning.

"There are some things for both of you. Downstairs in the back room. I'll bring them up." He left them to dispose of the clutter of medicine bottles on the bedside table and the rows of get-well cards fanned cheerfully across the top of the dresser. Was on the verge of men-tioning the housecoat in the bathroom, but changed his mind. On his way out of the room, he heard Andrea mutter, "Wouldn't you think he'd have noticed?"

He had noticed. Ever since the day the ambulance took Margaret to the hospice, where she grew small and faint in the company of caring strangers, the essence of her had been leaving the house like wisps of smoke swirling through the rooms and up the chimney.

When he watched Andrea walk toward her departure gate the next morning with her duffel bag and her mother's big suitcase, Frank was washed with a guilty sense of relief that she was carrying a remnant of Mar-garet away for safekeeping.

That night, unable to face the last of the leftover sandwiches, he pulled dinner #1 from the freezer. *La-sagna*, the label said. When he peeled off the carefully crimped foil, a note was taped to the plastic wrap inside.

Frank. Remember our first anniversary? We had lasagna and two bottles of Chianti at Stromboli's and came home and made love on the back lawn in the moonlight. I think that's my most beautiful memory of us.

He put the lasagna in the fridge, retrieved the burgundy velour robe that had remained undetected on the back of the bathroom door, and burying his face in Margaret's smell that always reminded him of peaches, he wept into the soft fabric.

Much later, with only the pool of moonlight on the floor lighting the kitchen, he heated the lasagna and filled two glasses with wine. He finished his own with the meal, then carried Margaret's glass to the bedroom, and set it on the bedside table. When he got up in the morning, the glass was empty, his mouth foul with the taste even though he couldn't remember during which of the long hours he'd finally sat up in bed and read until the words began to blur.

On Frank's first day back at school, his colleagues circled around, winding him tightly in the threads of their sympathy. Even the grade nines who filed into his math classes were solemn and tentative. The only time during the day that the cloth of all those murmured condolences loosened was when a chunky black woman in a nurse's uniform knocked on the door frame after his last class. For a split second Frank thought it was one of the hospice nurses, come to tell him Margaret had taken a bad turn.

"Mr. Murray? I'm Callista Darwell's mom."

He blinked at her. Her liquorice-coloured hair was so perfectly streaked with silver it looked as though the strands had been painted into the wild dustmop of a ponytail. She offered a half smile, showing a gap between her front teeth. Just like her daughter's.

"You phoned? And asked me to come talk to you about Callista's math?"

"Of course. Yes. Come in." He pulled the chair away from his desk and motioned her to it, perching himself on top of one of the student desks.

"Sorry I'm late. I just got off work. Didn't even get home to change."

"Oh, no problem." But there was a problem. A big problem with Callista's inability to do math, and her sullen refusal to do anything about it. For the ten minutes it took to discuss the implications of finishing grade nine with a seventeen per cent mark in math, Frank forgot about the ache in the back of his throat. That feeling of someone tapping an endless tune with a wooden mallet.

"Would it be a good idea to get her a tutor or something?"

He was torn between telling this woman that she'd be wasting her money, and fanning the little flame of hope. He'd expected Callista's mother to either rant at him for his failure to get through to her daughter, or to tell him that it didn't matter because Callista wasn't bound for academic glory.

"That would be a good first step, I think."

She shifted in the chair, her thighs straining against the pale blue pants. "Do you know someone I could call? I don't suppose you do that kind of thing?" Long ago he'd tutored almost every night of the week because they'd needed the extra income, but now? His expenses were reduced to utilities and food for one. Even groceries would be minimal with that freezer full of meals. "I'm afraid not, but our bulletin board has some phone numbers." He couldn't imagine Callista slouched at his kitchen table, and as soon as he invoked the image of his home, all he wanted was to get in his car and go. To pull out a couple of beers and settle down in front of the television. Tonight's meal was thawing on the counter. Turkey dinner—leftovers from Easter he suspected, because by Thanksgiving Margaret had stopped cooking. Andrea had come home and served a lentil casserole.

Frank walked Callista's mother to the front door to show her the board where some local tutors had hung their advertising. She randomly pulled off strips of telephone numbers, then offered him her hand.

"Thanks. I guess. Not what I wanted to hear but better now than when it's too late."

Frank felt a twinge of guilt. It was beyond late. If he'd called in the fall when it was already glaringly obvious that Callista was floundering, there might have been hope. But he'd rushed home every night because his wife was dying, and who could blame him for that?

On a day in February, Frank unwrapped a package of beef stroganoff. There seemed to be a pattern to the frequency of messages inside the foil. Once a week, he was to hold a frost-filmed paper in his hand and Margaret's voice would ring in his ears. He was tempted to ignore her numerical system, just once to step out of order and grab a package from the right hand side of the freezer, but the earnest determination of Margaret's neat black numbers kept him faithful.

Remember the night we had stroganoff at Sandra and Gerry's and they went into the kitchen to get the coffee and dessert and had that horrible fight? We snuck away and the next time we saw them they acted as though nothing had happened. Poor Sandra. She's had lousy luck with men. I never told you she was married before Gerry, did I? I expect the two of you will find each other for company, and I hope you do. But I have to admit that just thinking about it has made me so jealous I can hardly bear to talk to Sandra these days.

While the stroganoff heated, he sat for a while, then turned his attention to the pile of mail on the table and found a note from the cleaning lady.

Mr. Murray. Do you want me to throw out the dead plant in the living room?

He supposed that now that he was alone, he really didn't need anyone to clean, but it seemed like more effort to phone and cancel than it did to write the cheque once a month and leave it on the kitchen counter. He settled into Margaret's wicker rocking chair, and with an outstretched finger touched the last leaf remaining on the skeleton of the *ficus benjamina* and watched it drop into the pot with the withered remains of the rest of the plant. Margaret had never been good with plants, although she'd claimed to have a green thumb. For years a Boston fern had hung in the living room, bits of brown frond drifting to the floor whenever anyone passed too close. The pot of soil was probably still in a corner of the basement. Frank made a mental note to empty the storage room on the weekend.

Frank set the ficus, pot and all, next to the garbage can in the back alley.

The next day when he stopped at Safeway for milk, he impulsively picked up a small pot of ivy for the kitchen table.

Sandra had called almost every day for the first two weeks after Margaret died, then less frequently, and after Frank clumsily declined two invitations to supper, she stopped calling altogether. But the day after Frank bought the ivy, the mailman brought the March issue of *Bon Appetit*, and Frank finally remembered, just before he threw it in the recycling bin, that Margaret and Sandra had shared subscriptions to many magazines. Hoping she wouldn't ask what he'd done with *Chatelaine*, *Canadian Living* and *Canadian Gardener*, he walked up the street and folded the magazine into her mailbox.

When the doorbell rang at nine o'clock he was tempted to ignore it, but because he was so obviously at home, the lights on, the car in the driveway, he ran his hand through his hair, took a quick drink from the mug of cold coffee to mask the Scotch on his breath and opened the door.

Sandra was on the step, rosy-cheeked, the hood of her black parka sparkling with snowflake stars. Sometime after Frank's trip to her mailbox, a feathery blanket had fallen. "It's such a perfect winter night I decided to go for a walk." She batted at the flakes on her sleeve.

A couple of years ago, on just such a night, Sandra

had rung the bell and cajoled Margaret out into the snow with her. They had set out giddy, and returned an hour later, deep in serious conversation, to sit a long time over tea at the kitchen table. Frank was outside cleaning the driveway when Sandra left. He'd walked to the corner with her, watched until the lights came on in her dark house.

"Is Gerry out of town again?" he'd asked when he stomped his feet on the mat at the back door.

"Oh for gawd sake, Frank!" Margaret piled the mugs on the counter and shook her head. "Gerry's always out of town. This time Sandra isn't taking him back." He didn't bother to ask her why he should be expected to know these things. But he did wonder if Sandra was as cognizant of the details of their life as Margaret was of hers and Gerry's.

It all seemed so long ago, back then when they were couples. And now, here was Sandra with snowflakes in her hair, looking as though she wanted him to invite her inside and all he could say was, "I'd ask you in for coffee, but it's been a long day and I was on my way to bed."

"It's all right," she said. "I was just thinking about Margaret the whole time I was walking and how much I miss her and then of course I thought about you and the light was on and I wanted to stop. To make sure you were okay, you know?"

"Yes," he said. "Yes, I know." He wanted to open his arms and hug Sandra out there on the step, her coat wet with the smell of snow, but he could still feel the cold damp paper of Margaret's last note on his fingers.

On a night in March, Frank unwrapped a package of chili.

Chili's one of Michael's favourites, Frank. I had to stop in the middle of cooking and sit a while because I was so sad to think of leaving Michael and Andrea. Not meeting the people they marry or holding my grandchildren. Please keep reminding Michael that he needs to go back to school. What kind of a future is there in working as a lifeguard? You could have a good chat with him if you ask him to come over tomorrow night and share this. Just stick it in the fridge and open a can of soup for tonight. Or make an omelette. I haven't forgotten that you're capable of feeding yourself.

Michael scraped up the last bite of chili with a crust of bread. "Andy says I should convince you to get rid of these frozen dinners." He pushed away his empty dish. "Might be a good idea. Every time I come home and smell the food, I think Mom's going to walk out of the kitchen and hug me." He looked away, cleared his throat. "Sorry. I think I'm supposed to cheer you up." He seemed to be trying unsuccessfully to swallow, as though the bread had lodged in his throat. He blinked at Frank with bright eyes. "You know what's hardest to remember? That other smell. The one that's missing. Remember when I was a kid and you couldn't get me to quit coming into your bed in the middle of the night? I was scared and all it took to make me feel safe was that smell she had. Aw, Christ!" He rubbed his arm across his eyes and tried to smile. "She was always right here when we needed her. If I'm missing her this much, I can't imagine how hard it is for you, Dad."

Frank didn't try to answer. Instead, he opened two more beers and he and Michael moved into the living room to watch the hockey game. They never got around to discussing Michael's future.

The notes were becoming sporadic. Sometimes two or three a week. Often just the sort of reminders Margaret would have flung at him on his way out the door.

62. Cleaning-up-the-leftovers, or as Michael so eloquently dubbed it, Crap Casserole. Actually, I think you'll like this one because of the asparagus. Oh, and it's probably time to clean out the fridge. And don't forget to pick up a new filter for the furnace on your way home sometime soon.

Mostly benign but occasionally with a barbed end that was so typical of Margaret—fish hooks left dangling in their conversation.

79. Minestrone. If you haven't changed out of your school clothes yet, at least take off your sweater before you eat this soup. The last time I took your sweaters to the dry cleaners the woman asked if I had an elderly father!

Then two weeks would go by before he found another folded slip of paper. The dishes varied from his favourite Beef Bourguignon to the Deep Sea Surprise he'd never told her he disliked. But he kept hoping that somehow over the years she'd notice his lack of appetite for tuna.

84. Chicken stew. Pretty boring, eh? I didn't have interesting veg to add, and you always said the potatoes in stew had a texture that made you gag. You really were too fussy, Frank.

Frank was halfway through the meal before his

104

eyes rested on the empty chair across from him. He rewrapped the stew and slid the foil package into the garbage.

Andrea called at the beginning of April. "Daddy? I thought I'd come home for my birthday if that's okay with you."

The next morning when Frank skimmed through the paper while he ate his bowl of Shreddies, an ad for Theatre Calgary's presentation of Anne of Green Gables leapt off the page. He closed his eyes. Andrea, in a straw hat with red wool braids flying, danced in his memory. As she pirouetted on the front lawn, Margaret's hands caught hers, and then Michael's with his Dracula cape swirling, and the three of them whirled in the Halloween moonlight.

Margaret would have been on the phone, reserving tickets as soon as she knew their daughter was coming home. She would already have wrapped a pile of gifts. Frank wasn't sure he would have remembered Andrea's birthday if she hadn't called. He took down the calendar and circled November third with a thick red pen. Michael's birthday. Last year they'd eaten cake at the hospice.

Frank reserved two seats for *Anne of Green Gables*.

The night of the play, Andrea slid her arm through his on the way into the theatre. "Daddy, this is the nicest thing you could have done. A perfect birthday present."

At intermission, someone behind him in the lobby called, "Yo, Mr. Murray!" and he turned to Callista Darwell's gap-toothed smile. Her mother was beside her, hair tied back with a scarf dotted with tiny dan-

105

gling mirrors that twinkled when she swung her head. She looked slimmer in her tangerine-coloured pantsuit, more attractive than Frank remembered.

Since she'd found a tutor, Callista's math mark had risen to forty-five percent. With only two months to go, Frank held his breath every time he marked her homework and exams.

"Callista." Frank nodded and smiled. "And Callista's mother. Enjoying the show?"

Callista rolled her eyes. "The tickets were my birthday present from my aunt."

Her mother shrugged. "We tried to trade them for tickets to a rock concert, but no luck. Actually, I'm loving this show." Her voice had a pleasing huskiness that Frank hadn't noticed, the last time they spoke. "And so is Callista even though she won't admit it." He had to lean toward her to hear over the din of the lobby. When she shifted to put a playful arm around Callista, he caught a scent as warm and sweet as fresh bread.

As Andrea made her way back from the washroom, Callista and her mom moved to the line-up for drinks, and Frank felt oddly disappointed that he hadn't had the chance to introduce his beautiful daughter. Standing close to Mrs. Darwell, trying desperately to remember her first name, he'd felt like a dowdy old man.

Andrea nodded in the direction of the bar. "Who on earth was that?"

Callista turned just then and stared unabashedly at Andrea, hands on her hips. "One of my grade nines," Frank said. "And her mother."

After the intermission, Frank found it difficult to concentrate on the familiar story, his mind wandering

106

instead to a memory of reading to Andrea when she was a little girl in pink pyjamas. It was Margaret's choir night, and Andrea had insisted that he continue where her mother had left off in *Anne of Green Gables*. Now, glancing sideways, he saw a face as rapt as when he'd shared the story with her all those years ago.

For the rest of the play, Frank found himself scanning the audience, looking for the glint of tiny mirrors.

Andrea hadn't let him take out any frozen dinners while she was home. They ate out. With a sense of having fallen behind, when Michael stopped in a few days later, Frank gave him the four missed meals and five more he'd stockpiled because he'd begun accepting the occasional invitation to eat with Sandra. First, though, he checked for notes, and slipped the only one he found into his pocket. Michael went away happily swinging the bag of food, unaware of the Crap Casserole. There seemed to be an abundance of Clean-up-the-leftovers in the inventory. Still smiling, Frank unfolded the paper.

Baked beans, Frank. Remember the fall after Andrea was born? Every night for a week I set a can of beans on the table just before you got home and took Andrea out in her buggy until I was sure you'd eaten or gone out. You thought it was postpartum depression, didn't you? Actually, I found out about your little waitress friend. Surprise. I know it's cruel of me to do this, but I can't let you go on thinking that you got away with it. I would have told you eventually—some day when we were too old for it to matter—but I haven't the energy now to do it in person.

He tore the paper into tiny pieces and stuffed them down the garburetor with the beans. Then he made a cheese sandwich and sat outside on a sunny corner of the patio and tried, while he stared into the branches of the mayday tree that were just beginning to show buds, to conjure Nancy's face. He'd been teaching night school to make a little extra money so they could buy the house before the baby was born. Almost every night Nancy had lingered after class to ask for help. There was a bitterly cold night when he couldn't leave her standing at the bus stop. Then the ride home became a regular pattern. Then he'd gone in for a drink. He'd been flattered by the attention. He was a plain man, and a boring one he'd always thought as well. He wondered if Margaret knew that it was Nancy and not he who'd ended their affair. How long would it have taken him to return to his wife if the decision had been left to him? And how had Margaret found out?

When a cold wind stirred him, Frank stood up and was on his way inside when Sandra came around the corner of the house, a casserole dish in her hands, a bottle of wine protruding from her jacket pocket.

"I've been phoning," she said, "to see if you'd join me for supper. I knew you were home, because Michael stopped for a minute just to say hi. He said you were thawing something. He also said he had orders from Andrea to get you away from the deep freeze. So . . . here I am with Honey Mustard Chicken and a bottle of the corner store's best white plonk." She put a hand on his arm. "Am I being pushy, Frank? Just be honest if you'd rather be alone."

"No," he said. "I don't want to be alone."

He ignored the heavy wad of cheese sandwich in his stomach, and let Sandra help him prepare a salad, aware as he sliced tomatoes that here was Margaret's confidante. Here, mixing lemon juice and olive oil was a woman who probably knew more of his personal life than he himself understood. Sandra seemed as comfortable in this kitchen as if it were her own. She found the placemats and napkins Margaret saved for special occasions, the ceramic plate to go under the hot dish of chicken when she took it out of the oven.

At the table, Frank considered interrupting the companionable silence by asking Sandra how much she and Margaret had shared. If, when their voices dropped in the kitchen as he walked by the door, they had been cursing not only Gerry, but Frank, and all men for their infidelity.

When he looked up, Sandra's eyebrows were peaked, her head cocked to one side, a wave of blonde hair falling across her cheek. "What were you thinking about just then?" she asked.

He shrugged, tipped the wine to her glass, poured it half full, wiped the edge of the bottle with a napkin. "Just wondering what Margaret would say if she saw the two of us having dinner together. When you came around the corner, I felt as though she'd invited you herself."

Sandra's head moved back to centre, her chin high, a measuring look in her eyes. She picked up the glass and sipped. "I think she'd be happy, Frank." She sat up very straight and served the salad onto the two plates in front of her, then added a piece of chicken. This was Margaret's recipe. He'd pulled Honey Mustard Chicken from the freezer a week before. "She asked me to look out for you."

Frank took the plate she handed across the lush little pot of ivy in the centre of the table. "Oh. Well. It's good of you to do this. To bring over supper."

"I feel the same way about that freezer full of food as Andrea does." Wine glass to her lips once again, she paused. "I couldn't believe how determined Margaret was to put up exactly three hundred and sixty-five meals. I told her you'd be desperate for fresh food within a month."

He shrugged, looked down at the chicken on his plate. "Some things taste the same whether they're frozen or fresh."

"You're a good and loyal man, Frank Murray." She smiled and he noticed that she was wearing more make-up than usual. Her lashes were thicker, swept up so that her eyes looked wide. Lipstick a shade darker than the pink sweater that was scooped to show the soft swell of her breasts. Sandra had dressed for the occasion. She reached out a fingertip to the ivy. "Pretty." Then the smile faded. "Margaret tried and tried to get some ivy cuttings to grow. Not her thing, or mine. We were both better at cooking, which I guess is why she did what she did. She said it would give you a chance to gradually get used to her being gone."

Frank swallowed a bite of chicken. "I think," he said, "it was more a case of making me feel like she's still here."

Late in June, when Frank stopped at the grocery store on his way home from school, he arrived at the cashier to find himself staring at Callista Darwell's mother yet again. Annabel, the name tag said, but this time he'd recognized her before she remembered him. Not until he'd handed her his Visa card did she look at him with surprise.

"Mr. Murray. Sorry. I'm still new enough at this that I don't pay as much attention to the customers' faces as I should. How you doin'?"

"I thought you were a nurse," Frank said.

"Yeah, well, I seem to be in love with uniforms, don't I?" She grinned. "Never an RN. Only an assistant. I got tired of the nursing home. Heavy work, kinda depressing, and the shift work made it hard to keep track of Callista."

Ah yes, Callista. She was going to scrape through math after all. Just barely, but she would pass.

"She tell you she's going to summer school? Prep for grade ten math?"

Frank shook his head, not wanting to show his surprise but hoping Annabel Darwell would see approval in his face. Know that he was impressed that she was dedicated to hauling Callista out of bed for a whole month of math.

He was turning the cart full of grocery bags toward the door when she called to him softly, "Hey, Mr. Murray?" Frank looked back. "I never told you I'm sorry about your wife. I didn't know that day I came to see you at school that you'd just lost her. I'm sorry." And she truly did look sorry, her arms folded across her chest, her lips slightly parted, her attention totally focussed on him and not on the woman impatiently rearranging food on the conveyor belt.

Dinner that night was a single wrapped t-bone steak taped to the top of a package of peach cobbler.

Microwave a potato and throw together a little salad to have with the steak. It seems like a meal that needs dessert. These are the lovely peaches you brought home yesterday. They reminded me of that summer we ate our way through five pounds on the drive home from Kelowna. That night, you said making love to me was like eating a peach.

Frank didn't bother with baked potato or vegetables. He barbecued the steak and ate at the picnic table, the peach cobbler untouched on the kitchen counter, until the rising damp from the lawn and a plague of mosquitoes drove him inside.

In July, Sandra surprised Frank with tickets to the Calgary Folk Festival and they spent Saturday afternoon huddled together under an umbrella, sipping from Sandra's thermos of brandy-laced coffee. Finally, when the sky turn wickedly black, the air crackling with an approaching storm, the concert shut down and they ran the four blocks to Frank's car.

"Shall we try to find a warm restaurant willing to let us through the door in this condition?" he asked.

"No." The windshield was streaming with rain, the inside of the car muggy with their breath. She began to unbutton her wet jacket, then the blouse underneath. "There's not a chance anyone can see into this car even if they're foolish or unlucky enough to be out there. I'm freezing, Frank." He doubted this could be so, because her skin was a rosy pink. "Take off that wet shirt, and help me get warm." When he pulled her close, she was soft and moist against his chest. "And then we're going back to my place," she whispered, "and eventually I'll get around to finding us some food." It seemed to Frank that she had it all mapped out, that he hadn't any choice but to follow. She made it easy for him by leading the way.

Sandra, Frank discovered over three more months of shared meals and evenings together, was as bored with sports as Margaret had been, and had the same annoying habit of pretending to watch a game with him but talking incessantly. He begged off her invitation to watch the Grey Cup at her house with the excuse that he and Michael had never missed watching the game together.

"That's even better," she said. "I'll tell my two guys he's coming and they can join us with their girlfriends and we'll make it a party. Anyone else you can think of? The more the merrier, right?"

Wrong. Frank hated parties, and if Sandra didn't know this after all the years she'd spent in Margaret's company, Frank had totally misread the communication between the two of them. "No. Please don't do that. I'd rather keep it simple. If you like, we can go out for dinner afterward."

"Oh you." She pretended to pout. "I always thought Margaret was exaggerating when she said you'd turn into a hermit some day. Just so you know, I'm not going to let that happen. But I'll excuse you this once."

Fortunately, for the moment she did let up, and the

day went ahead as Frank hoped it would. Before Michael arrived, Frank went down to the freezer and filled two bags with the last of the dinners. In the kitchen, he carefully removed notes, and slipped them under the ivy which was now in serious need of a larger pot.

At half-time, Michael looked up from peeling the label on his bottle of Big Rock and exhaled through his teeth. "Dad, I'm on a snoop mission from Andrea. She says from talking to Sandra, she's picking up hints that you might surprise us with some kind of news at Christmas time. I guess Sandra told her she's been looking at condos now that Brad and Kelvin are both working and not likely to take over the basement again." He laughed. "Or maybe she just wants to make sure that doesn't happen. Anyway, you know how much Andy hates surprises. She's thinking you might have the same idea about wanting a smaller place. And then she was thinking maybe this was something the two of you were cooking up together. She knows you've been . . . "

Frank held up his hand. "Wait a minute! There are no surprises up my sleeve. Andrea comes by that aversion to surprise quite honestly, you know. Michael, I would never spring anything on you. I have no plans to change my residence or anything else for that matter, and I'll phone Andrea tonight and make that clear."

They watched the second half in silence, and then Michael took the bagful of dinners and left. Frank opened another beer and sat at the kitchen table, staring out the window into the early gloom. Finally, he idly moved the plant and picked up the notes. There was one reminder to get the carpets cleaned, then a note that suggested he must be tired of rattling around in the house alone. He threw that one aside and un-folded a third.

I've put this off till the bitter end but I'd better con-fess, because I'm afraid Sandra might tell you someday if I don't. I'm beginning to regret that she and I were so close, that we had no secrets. Still, because of that she's the best person for you.

I paid that girl to break up with you, Frank. I followed you to her apartment, and I went there the next day and told her she couldn't have you. That Andrea and I needed you more. I gave her five hundred dollars. I borrowed it from Andrea's education fund, and it took me four years of scrimping on grocery money to put it back. You ate a lot of cheap cuts to pay for your fling. But you're a good man, Frank. You've been worth every cent of it.

Frank swept the remaining paper from the table, put on a windbreaker and walked through a needle-like drizzle to Sandra's house. She answered the door in a grey sweatsuit trimmed with pink, a little breathless, her cheeks rosy.

"Hey, come in! Is the game over already? What a nice surprise! I was doing my exercises." She smiled. "Danc-ing mostly, and a partner would be lovely." From the living room, Joan Baez's rich Spanish reached him like a hot embrace.

"*Gracias a la Vida,*" Frank said.

"Right," Sandra grabbed his hand. "Here's to life! Take off your coat, Frank. It's a miserable night and I'm so glad to have company."

He shook his head. "I can't stay. I just wanted to ask you something."

She let her arm drop and took a step back. "Goodness. Sounds serious. Ask away."

"Did Margaret tell you I cheated on her long ago?"

She hesitated, brushed her hair back with both hands at her temples. "No." She shook her head. "You don't have to tell me this, Frank."

He could see the lie lurking behind her eyes. Margaret needn't have worried about Sandra's betraying her.

She was so close he could smell the heat of her dancing. Only a few weeks ago when he kissed her, he'd marvelled that in the autumn air she tasted of apples. A taste so reminiscent of Margaret he'd had difficulty catching his breath. There were times when she felt so familiar in his arms he expected to be looking into Margaret's gold-flecked eyes, and was startled by the soft blue. It would be so easy to replace Margaret with Sandra. She would sell her house, move in with him. Andrea and Michael would be pleased, because she was already like an aunt. Like Margaret's sister. One as skilful as the other at keeping secrets.

She lifted her palms to his cheeks. "Take your jacket off and stay a while," she whispered. "I don't care about what's past. Let's just get on with the future. Margaret would have forgiven you, I'm sure, and she'd be happy for what we have now."

But Frank was listening instead to Joan Baez, her segue into the next song. Caught up in a memory of Margaret in the kitchen, singing along with the scratchy tape deck. How many years ago was it? A Thursday night, he remembered, because she left for choir practice after dinner. Margaret humming her way to church

116

to a song about spending a whole night in a twin bed with a stranger.

"What's it called?" he'd asked her. He'd just come in from work.

"Hmm?" She'd looked up from the pot she was stirring, distracted, far away from the steamy kitchen.

"The song. I just wondered what you were thinking about, singing those words." And for a moment he did wonder. Carrying around the suitcase of guilt about his own affair, he'd never stopped to think that someday Margaret might be tempted to stray from the marriage.

She brushed a strand of hair off her cheek with the back of her hand. "Who pays any attention to the lyrics? They're just words. Pretty words. It's the melody I love."

When she left that evening, he'd found the plastic case for the tape. "Love Song to a Stranger." Such a sexy song. He'd played it over and over again that night, thinking about Nancy in her tiny apartment.

"Did Margaret give you the Joan Baez CD?" he asked Sandra now. "I wondered where it had gone."

"It was in the grey suitcase," she said. "I was supposed to give that back, wasn't I?"

"I think that would be a good idea," he said. "Giving back the suitcase."

"You mean now?" Sandra shook her head. "I don't understand, Frank. What's wrong? Things are going so well between us. Why . . . ?"

He trudged home through the rain carrying the empty suitcase. He'd order a pizza tonight, he decided. He had papers to mark, and that reminded him suddenly of Callista Darwell and he wondered if she was failing miserably in someone else's class, or if a major miracle had occurred. He thought he might offer to tutor her the next time he saw her mom. Annabel Darwell was bound to turn up again.

Frank tilted his head to a snowlit sky, the first flake falling like a wet kiss on his cheek.

BURNED

Val had just picked her way through a gang of kids in the parking lot of the housing project and was fumbling for her key when the door in the adjoining unit flew open. A young woman, thin as a pencil, with a long neck and a head of greenish blonde tufts more like feathers than hair, stepped out.

The genius who built the place had set the doors side by side so that every two units shared a front step and sidewalk. Handy when it came to removing snow, but Val had yet to have a neighbour who owned a shovel. This had to be the new neighbour Josh had been yakking about, and she didn't look promising in the snow shovel department either.

"Hey, you're Josh's mom, right?"

Just once Val wanted to come home and put her feet up without answering to the world for her son. She set the bags of groceries on the concrete step and folded her arms across the front of her tired uniform. "That's me."

119

This little gal was wearing a uniform too. A frilly apron over a black skirt that just covered her ass, and a black and white polka dot blouse with *Chrissy* stitched on the left breast pocket. She looked almost as young as Josh. Not at all what Val had expected. She'd envisioned someone more like the poster on the inside of Josh's closet door.

"There's two little kids and a . . . a girl," Josh had mumbled the day the new people moved in. His ears glowed red, and he frowned. He'd run out to snoop when he saw the U-haul backing up to the townhouse, and rattled his skateboard up and down the parking strip while they unloaded. Since then, Val had worked eight straight days and by the time she got home from a shift at the nursing home she wasn't interested in jumping on the Welcome Wagon.

"Does he babysit?"

Two little boys were scrapping in the hallway behind their mom, the older one whaling away at the baby with a stuffed toy. The little one, dressed in undershirt and diaper, snapped at his brother's heels like a terrier.

"Josh?" Val felt her eyebrows take flight. It was only a few months since she'd reluctantly given her son a key instead of sending him to her sister's after school. She had nightmares about coming home to a smoldering square of rubble. "Oh no. He's never looked after a baby."

"Well, does he want to?"

Val blew out a long breath and shook her head. "He hasn't been around many little kids. And he has a lot of homework." She could imagine the look on the math teacher's face if Josh told him he couldn't study because he had a job.

The girl stared at Val through circles of green eye shadow, oblivious to the baby who'd toddled onto the sidewalk and was making tracks for the street. His dragging diaper looked fully loaded. Val pointed, and Chrissy gave a swift shove between the other boy's shoulder blades.

"Travis, go get your brother!" The older kid sprang into action, hauling the baby back by the armpits. The mom put her hands on her hips. "I'd pay him good, and I won't be too late. I'm kinda desperate here."

"You mean right now?" Val glanced at her own door. She could hear the electronic racket of Nintendo. Josh was battling his way past the Big Boss of some mythical empire.

"No, my mom looks after them when I'm at work. I need him Saturday." The baby had pulled himself up on her leg and clung to the hem of the apron. "I don't know any sitters around here and I'll go nuts if I don't get a night off." When she peeled his fingers free, the little guy plopped onto the cement without a whimper. "I'm Tonya, by the way."

Val stared at the stitching on the pocket.

"Oh yeah," Tonya flicked at the *Chrissy* with a shimmery green fingernail. "I always make up a name for work. Otherwise some jerk'll try to find you at home."

"Not a problem where I work," Val said. Her own *Valerie* was tucked into her pocket. "Look, how about we let you know tomorrow? I'll talk it over with Josh."

In the time it took Val to haul the last of the groceries to the door, her neighbour had thrown jackets on the kids, loaded them into a double-wide stroller and was running toward the bus stop.

Val stepped into the gloom of her living room. The drapes were closed and Josh sat cross-legged on the floor an arm's length from the television. The air was hot with the stench of microwave popcorn.

"Hey! Some help with the bags would be a good thing if you're expecting to eat tonight."

"In a minute. I'm in the middle of something tricky."

"What else is new?" she muttered, carrying one bag down the short hall to the kitchen but leaving the rest for Josh.

More than half of the kernels were charred into the popcorn wrappings on the cluttered table. Josh had cleared a small square of arborite and scrawled with a felt pen: *call dad rit now.*

No. Not right now. Val pulled a litre of Coke out of the grocery bag, filled a glass with ice cubes, poured, sat down at the table and dragged another chair forward for her feet. Josh's lunchbag was on the counter where she'd left it for him this morning. Or was it the same one he'd forgotten yesterday?

Her eyes were closed, her cheek pressed to the cool glass when Josh wandered in. He dug around in the grocery bag, pulled out a package of wieners and ripped it open with his teeth.

"Aw Josh! Not raw! Those are crawling with bacteria!"

He shrugged and stuffed the meat into his mouth. "Did you call Dad?"

"Give me a break, kiddo. I just got in the door and my feet feel like ground beef." She waggled her hand at the bag on the counter. "If that's yesterday's, you'd better get it out to the garbage before it walks. So you didn't have lunch?"

"Devin gave me some of his."

"Healthy stuff, right? Chips and pop? Did you take your pills?"

He dropped the phone into her lap. "Dad says it's important."

She flicked through the call display. Three from Jerry, one from the Calgary Board of Education, and one from Blockbuster Video. "What's the school calling about?"

"Gee, I don't know." Josh crinkled up his pale blue eyes and edged toward the door. He had a new crop of pimples on his chin. Life was not giving this kid any breaks. "I gotta finish my game." When she grabbed at the back pocket of his jeans, he deked sideways, then dodged into the living room.

She knew she should go after him, but she'd used up the last of her patience on an old woman who insisted she was Katherine Hepburn and for the third time this week had called a cab to take her to the Palliser hotel because Spenser Tracy was meeting her there. At least Josh knew who he was, and so did Val, although there were times when flying off to cuckoo land seemed a damn sight easier than protecting her kid from himself.

"Take your pills!" she shouted after him. "And bring those groceries in here!"

Jerry was as predictable as ever. "Look, Val, I can't have the kid this weekend. I got an out-of-town job. How about we skip this once and I'll pick him up in two weeks."

She curled her tongue over her front teeth. The icy cold pop had set up a dull ache in that cavity she was trying to ignore. "Maybe it's just as well. He's got a job for Saturday night. What do you think about Josh babysitting?"

"Why not? When I was fourteen I was helping my dad on a construction site."

"This job doesn't come with a hammer. We've got a new neighbour with two kids. You'd trust Josh with a baby?"

"How hard can it be to look after a baby for a couple of hours?"

Val raised the glass of ice cubes to her forehead. "You wouldn't let him have a puppy because it was too much responsibility."

"That was a couple of years ago, Val. Give the kid a break."

"Does that mean you're getting him a dog for your place?"

He hung up on her. She imagined the look on Josh's face when she told him his dad was bailing again. But maybe Jerry was right about giving Josh a break. She'd pretend she didn't get the message from the school if they called back tomorrow. Today's call from the guidance counselor would be no different from yesterday's. Josh had spent lunch hour in the office. A problem with a couple of other kids. Not his instigating, but he "responded inappropriately." Meaning he'd either decked someone or ripped the door off a locker. Tomorrow she'd be here to make sure he took his Ritalin before he left the house.

Blockbuster Video was calling to tell her there was

a Nintendo game outstanding by two weeks. That one didn't need a call-back either.

She swung her feet onto the floor. Tomorrow was the start of her three-day weekend and by God she'd earned every second of it. Tonight she was barricading herself in the bathroom with a tubful of bubbles and a good book. Meanwhile, though, there was still supper to throw on the table and the grizzly battle of homework after that.

She'd been prepared for a flat refusal when Josh heard Tonya's offer, or an indifferent shrug and a quick return to Mortal Kombat, but not for the big-eyed whoop of delight.

"Really? Oh man, that would be sweet! Devin baby-sits and he makes mega-bucks every weekend."

"Devin? Oh, well then." Why would she worry about Josh if someone, anyone had entrusted a child to Devin? He was Josh's only friend, but Val wouldn't have given Devin responsibility for a turnip.

The next day after school, Val sent Josh to tell Tonya he could sit for her on Saturday night. When supper was ready and he still wasn't back, she went out and rang the bell. Josh answered, with the baby on his hip, the three-year-old, Travis, wrapped around his leg, and a grin that stretched from one blushing ear to the other.

"Tonya wanted me to stay and get to know the kids. We're like hanging out in the living room, building stuff while she takes a break."

"Two hours should be plenty. You look like a pro. Supper's ready."

"Yeah, but Tonya's sleeping, and Travis says they're

hungry and he wants me to make grilled cheese. Only there's no cheese and no bread. Do you think I should open a can of soup?"

"I think their mom can make their supper."

Same floor plan as her place. Val scooped up the kids, one on each arm, and stomped up the stairs to the master bedroom. She banged on the door with her knee, then cracked it open just enough to herd the kids through. "Josh is coming home for supper now, Tonya. Bye bye!" When the two little bodies made a beeline for the bed, she closed the door and went downstairs. Josh stood in the hallway trying to spin a beach ball on his index finger.

"Did she say anything about paying you for today?" Val asked as she pulled him out Tonya's door and back through their own.

She'd been cleaning the bathroom when he left and hadn't noticed that he'd changed into his khakis and button-up shirt. His hair was different too. Instead of swooping low over his forehead, it was spiked into a ridge from hairline to crown. He looked painfully like a rooster.

"No, but she says she'll pay me five bucks an hour tomorrow night. Only she won't be able to give it to me till pay-day."

"We'll see," Val said. "Let's eat."

Through the thin kitchen wall, they could hear wailing and the slam of cupboard doors in the townhouse next door. "You really want to babysit?"

"For sure! Those kids really like me, Mom." The truculent set of his jaw softened and he looked so vulnerable that the back of Val's throat tightened.

126

"The baby fell asleep on my lap when we were watching TV. Tonya said I could take them to the playground for a while tomorrow night before I put them to bed."

Over her dead and bleeding body. "No way. That's too much responsibility, Josho. What if one of them took off in one direction and the other went the other way? Or what if they fell off the slide? Or those punks who hang around in the evening started hassling you?"

He put his elbows on the table and hunched over the plate. When he slurped up the spaghetti dangling from his fork it left a ring of sauce around his lips. He frowned. "I guess. Can I bring them over here for a while and show them my models? I could take my Nintendo along."

That evening Josh dug through the bottom of his closet and filled an old gym bag with GI Joe action figures, the stuffed dolphin he'd spent twenty bucks "winning" at the Stampede, and a couple of rusted Tonka trucks.

He sorted through the movies, pursing his lips and following the words with his finger as he read the boxes. Just before he slid the pile into his bag, he discarded Bambi. "This is too scary for little kids." He shuddered. "I hate that part where Bambi's mom gets trapped in the forest fire."

Val was flipping pancakes the next morning when Tonya phoned.

"Look, I'm not gonna need Josh tonight after all. My girlfriend's niece is coming over."

"So you want him for next Saturday maybe?"

"No, I don't think so."

Val stuck her head around the corner. Josh was glued to the television. She took the phone into her bedroom and stared out the window and across the fence at Tonya's postage stamp of a yard. An over-turned trike lay in the dirt.

"You want to pay him for the two hours he looked after your kids yesterday then?"

There was a crash, a five second pause, and then a scream that could've shattered glass. "Oh shit! Just a minute!"

When Val leaned against the window she could see into Tonya's kitchen. A shadow swooped across the room. Within seconds there was an unmistakable smack and then wailing in stereo, the slam of a door and finally Tonya was back. Now the crying was more audible through the bedroom wall than through the phone.

"I'll pay him when I have some cash. He's a nice kid and everything but I was talking to my girlfriend last night and she says I'm nuts to let a guy look after my kids. She told me some babysitting stories about teenage boys that made me want to puke."

"Then you tell him you don't need him. Just a minute." Val clamped her hand over the phone, walked into the living room and held it out to Josh. "Tonya wants to talk to you." He sprang up from the floor in front of the TV and grabbed the phone, his whole body thrumming. Looking as though she'd handed him a gift-wrapped box as big as a bus. When his shoulders sagged, and his responses turned to dead monosyllables, Val couldn't listen, and left the room.

As she stepped into the kitchen, the smoke detector

went off. By the time she ran the griddle onto the back step and scraped the charred pancakes into the garbage, Josh had climbed up on the table and ripped the battery out of the alarm.

Val closed the door, leaving the pan to smoke outside. "There's a way to turn that off without destroying it."

His arm flew back. The battery ricocheted off the oven door. "Stupid cow!" He grabbed Val's coffee cup from the table.

"Whoa!" She snatched the mug from his fist. "Talk. Don't break things. What did she say?"

"She said she doesn't need me to babysit 'cause she got her friend's kid or somebody."

"And?"

"And that sucks and it's a load of crap." He turned away and swiped at his nose with his pyjama sleeve. "Yesterday she said nobody from her old neighbourhood would come all the way over here."

Val walked around to stand in front of him. "Why do you think she changed her mind?"

His face was red, the eruption on his chin even more inflamed and the rims of his eyes swelling. "Somebody told her I'm stupid." He shrugged, his lips wobbling. "Maybe she talked to somebody who goes to my school and she doesn't want a dummy looking after her kids."

Val followed Josh when he ran into the living room and threw himself face down on the couch. She sat beside him and rubbed his back, gently kneading the fragile knobs of his spine. "That's not it, Josh. She doesn't know you at all. Not at all."

He snorted into the worn tweed of the couch and

129

turned his red face toward her. "She's not so smart herself. Did you see how she spells her name?"

As always, she laughed to keep from crying. "Yeah, kiddo, I noticed that too." She rumpled his hair.

When he finally pushed himself to sitting and pulled his knees to his chest, Val got up and slid a tape in the video recorder. "You wanna forget about pancakes and go somewhere for lunch instead?"

"I thought we were broke until pay-day."

"We'll look under some cushions and see what we can scrape together. I'm not ready to go anywhere for a while. Let's watch *Bambi*."

They sat side by side on the couch. When they got to the forest fire part, Val felt Josh's shoulder tight against hers.

WATER FROM THE WELL

Soon Marta will be here to slide the pins from the coiled braid at the nape of my neck. Her fingers will fan the pleated grey waves across my back. "Mutti!" she will say. How long since they washed your hair?"

Ilsa was marooned, perched on a green vinyl chair that sucked at her thighs where her dress was hitched crooked beneath her. She'd awakened with Marta on her mind. She whispered her daughter's name to the stiff-fingered rhythm of the knitting needles. The names of all her children: Marta, Walter, Annaliese, Bruno. The living and the dead. Not sure if she chanted them aloud, or in her thoughts, until the Filipino nursing aide poked her head into the room and asked, "You calling for me, Ilsa? Or is Bernice making all that racket?"

Before she could answer that it was the one in the other bed moaning and carrying on as though she was dying, someone else stepped through the door.

131

"What are you knitting now, Oma? Slippers or scarf?" The tall girl brushed snow off her shoulders.

"Jeannie." Ilsa tried to blink the sticky webs from her brain. "I thought you were coming in the morning."

"It is still morning, but you've probably been up since dawn. Did you have a good sleep?"

"With that one jabbering?" She pointed over her shoulder with the free knitting needle, stabbing into the air on the other side of the room. "Since she came, who can sleep?"

"Water, please." The voice from the bed sounded like fingernails on a screen.

"See what I put up with? Always complaining about something." She frowned at a dropped stitch many rows back, and put the wool aside. "No school today?"

The girl pressed a cold cheek to hers. "School? Oma, don't make me a little girl again. I'm on my way to work. At the bank, remember?"

Now the voice from the other bed commenced a low keening. The old woman lay scattered in the bed like the broken limbs of a tree, her hair sprouting from her skull in tufts that looked as though they would blow away with a puff of breeze.

"Be quiet!" Ilsa shouted.

Her granddaughter shushed her. "What is it with you and Mrs. Ridley? You know, you talk just as much as she does."

"I?" Steadying herself with a hand on the night table, she stood up tall in her stout black shoes. They tried to make her wear bedroom slippers in this place. As though she had nowhere to go. "I mind my own business," she said. "I'm a quiet woman waiting here patiently to die." She tugged at the back of her skirt, pulling the wrinkled fabric free of her damp skin. *Someone has stolen my garter belt and stockings again. Marta will have to go to the Army and Navy store.*

While her granddaughter unwound a scarf as bright as buttercups, Ilsa stooped to hoist a water jug from the floor. Shuffling the few steps to the mahogany dresser—her only piece of home—she tested the soil in the pots of African violets, then tipped the pitcher to each, careful to avoid drips on the hairy leaves. She shoved the pitcher out of sight between the chair and the nightstand where two more jugs stood.

"Should you be doing that?" Jeannie asked. "Walking on your own?"

"Am I on my own? I thought you were here?" The effort of easing back into the chair, of concealing her pain, squeezed the breath from her chest.

Mrs. Ridley flicked open a milky eye. "I need a drink, please. A drink of water." The claw that reached over the blue blanket plucked at the air as though clutching at feathers.

Jeannie took a step toward Mrs. Ridley, her gaze swinging from one surface to the next and then finally descending to the hiding spot. "Oma!" She swooped toward the stainless steel water jugs.

"No!" Ilsa's arm blocked her, but before they could resolve the standoff, the door whooshed open.

"Good morning, ladies." Here was the fat nurse, the one who looked, Marta always said, like she'd been sucking on a radish.

"Bernice? Let's go listen to some lovely carols." No

answer from the lump in the next bed. Her eyes had fallen shut again. Only the twitch of fingers at the hem of her sweater gave her away. Mrs. Ridley. Bernice, in this place.

It puzzled Ilsa still to have her own name tossed around like a child's toy. Ilsa, Ilsa. Like the bounce of a bright red ball. Good morning, Ilsa. Time for bed, Ilsa. Nice chicken for lunch today, Ilsa. For eighty-eight years she'd owned that name, but could count on her fingers the people who'd used it in her adult life. Even to her friends, she was Mrs Gartner. Mrs. Rolf Gartner, so there would be no mistake.

The first time Marta heard, she'd stormed to the nurse's desk. Her voice was so loud it carried down the hall and back into the room. "My mother's name is Mrs. Gartner."

She'd come back to the room with a roll of tape, covered "Ilsa" on the name plate at the end of her bed and printed MRS. GARTNER in big black letters. But still, she was Ilsa in this place. And did it really matter?

Mrs. Ridley—Bernice—was carted off moaning to listen to the Sunday school children sing. Poor little ones never knew what to do, where to look, when the moaners sang along.

Jeannie held aloft the bag she'd carried in. "I brought you something new." Shaking the wrinkles from a pink shirt, and then pants, she draped them over her grandmother's knees.

"What is this? Pyjamas?"

"No, for daytime. Fleece pants and a top. Very cosy and they won't get wrecked in the laundry like your good dresses."

134

Marta washes my dresses. Folds them every Sunday into a bag and brings them back on hangers on Wednesday. And my underthings, hand washed in Ivory soap, not thrown in a boiling machine with the smelly garments of strangers.

"Your mother takes my clothes."

Jeannie knelt in front of her, crossing the arms of the shirt, tucking the cuffs one inside the other, and then finally looking up into her eyes. "Oma, Mom's been gone for six months. I can't do your laundry."

"Who said you should? Just tell them to put my name in this new suit. Every day since that one came," she jerked her chin at Mrs. Ridley, "I have to go into her closet and find the clothes she steals."

"I talked with the nurses last week. They said your clothes are in your own closet. They say you're the one who's been snitching things."

"I?" She sniffed, but let Jeannie take her hand. "What do they know?"

"Are they treating you well, Oma?" She sounded so sad, little Jeannie, but at the same time she sounded like her mother. She would stand up to the sour-faced nurse when the need arose.

"They do their job." Ilsa shook her head. What could she say about living among strangers? "They come and go and when they're here they worry about what's happening at home. You should hear Marcella, the little Filipino girl, how she talks about her family." Yesterday when she'd changed the sheets, Marcella had cried about her sister back home dying of cancer and no one to take her babies. She would have to go back to the Philippines herself, she said. "Likely even the fat one has troubles. How can we know what goes on in other people's lives?"

Jeannie poked a wrist free of the heavy cuff on her jacket and looked at her watch. "I'm sorry to be in such a hurry, but I have to be at work at ten o'clock. Uncle Walter said he'd pop in this afternoon. Shall I take you to the lounge before I leave?"

Ilsa patted the fleecy pile on the bed. "I should maybe wear my lounging suit to go there?" Peering over the top of the wire frames, she let her glasses slide down her nose and looked up at the girl, coaxing a grin that reminded her more of the boys, of Walter and Bruno, than of Marta. Never before had she seen the old man in Jeannie's eyes, but there he was smiling at her over his basket of apples where they stood together on the dock waiting for the big ships.

"Oma?" *The hand covered hers like a shy glove. "Ilsa Reinhold. Someday we'll sail," Rolf said. And so we did, but he landed me on a poor prairie farm with no well. Nor an apple nor an ocean in sight.*

"Oma? Shall I wheel you to the lounge?"

"Lounge? Who has time to lounge?" *Run to the garden and bring an onion and parsley for the soup.* Her eyes were drawn to the window, to coloured bulbs strung on the juniper bushes. Christmas already? *We should roll the springerle today.*

Marta is holding both hands now, squeezing, forgetting that my knobbled bones are held together by sharp pins. Ilsa winced and pulled away.

"Oh, I'm sorry, Oma. I forgot about your poor hands. Look, I have to go but I'll see you tomorrow. Christmas Eve, remember? The Handi-Bus is bringing

136

you to Walter and Lydia's. I'll make sure you get on, then follow you over."

Marta is making Weihnnachten. Not Lydia!

Ilsa pushed away the hand on her arm. She felt the gentle kiss on her cheek, the rush of air when the door opened and closed, then she was alone. The shake of her head drip-dropped tears onto her wrists.

When she stirred, her neck was stiff from the lopsided sleep in the ugly chair. Mrs. Ridley was back. From across the room she heard snoring. *Who brought that one here? Let her into the house?*

"Ilsa? What are you doing, sleeping in the middle of the morning?" Marcella bent to her chair, eyes bright like a sparrow's. "Time for lunch."

The fat one came through the door. "Take Bernice," she said. "I'll bring Mrs. Gartner." She pulled the curtain that divided the room, manoeuvred the wheelchair round and offered an arm as strong as any man's. When Ilsa was seated, the nurse eased her own big bottom onto the green chair. "Your granddaughter says you're unhappy. That you want a different roommate."

From the other side of the curtain, Mrs. Ridley's moans and Marcella's encouraging chirps carolled the move from bed to chair and then out the door. A tide of voices in the hall rolled toward the smell of lunch, toward cream soup that hung from the spoon like wallpaper paste.

"What is it about Mrs. Ridley that's bothering you? You shared so nicely before with poor Mary . . . "

Snowflakes as big as fists clumped down outside the window. Or maybe just her glasses needed cleaning.

137

She pulled them off with a shaky hand, one temple catching in her hair. When she reached up to free it from behind her ear her fingers puzzled at the bristly fringe on her neck. *Mary? What is this woman talking about? There is no Mary here.*

"So there's nowhere to move you. You understand that, don't you? These little problems between you and Mrs. Ridley will work out in the end."

Oh, yes. Mrs. Ridley. She was to share her room with Mrs. Herbert Ridley. She slid her glasses onto her nose and stared into the pale eyes of the nurse. "In the end?" she said. "You mean when one of us dies?" Then she folded her arms, put her feet securely on the rests of the wheelchair and waited for the fat one to take her to her lunch.

In the afternoon there were more visitors. Little girls trooping through the halls with flowers. This time both she and Mrs. Ridley had been shuttled from the dining room to the lounge, part of the sea of shipwrecked grey faces bobbing in their wheelchairs. In the drab room, the children were like bright cut-outs pasted onto a yellowed old photo.

When they were wheeled back to their room to nap, there was a poinsettia on Mrs. Ridley's bedside table. Marcella held up a handmade card and waved it in front of Mrs. Ridley's nose. "See, a nice present for you, Bernice. Merry Christmas from the 203 Brownie pack." She picked a paper thimble of pills off the tray she'd carried in, then frowning, looked from the night table to the dresser. "Jesus in the garden! Your water's gone again."

138

Ilsa steered her chair to the window. The snow had stopped and on the street a long line of cars inched toward the traffic light at the corner. *The old man won't drive to the city. He scarcely leaves his bedroom now. The only way I can visit with Marta or Walter is to catch a ride with a neighbour.*

This morning she'd left her Bible on the window ledge, and she reached for it now.

"Ilsa, did you hide the water again?"

She absent-mindedly fingered the skein of wool in the pocket on the side of her wheelchair, ignoring the nurse rummaging around the room. *If I double the yarn it will make warm mittens for Bruno.*

There was a metallic clink behind her. "Bernice can't hardly get out of bed never mind play hide-and-seek when she's thirsty. Now you stop this, you hear?" Marcella's footsteps moved round the bed, and she began to cajole Mrs. Ridley to swallow. Then the scolding tone warmed. "Look, Ilsa, here's your son."

"Hi, Mom." The man crouched in front of her chair. He tapped the Bible that lay open on her lap. "A bit of evening devotion?"

She blinked through the snow in front of her eyes. Here was Walter with a gift-wrapped package. "I brought chocolates for the nurses," he said. He set the box on the floor and dug in the pocket of his overcoat. "For you, some peppermints. You can suck them while you pray."

"I'm praying for patience to put up with that one. Listen to her yammering again about water." She tapped the cover of the Bible. "Someone asked today how long since my husband's gone, so I'm looking. I wrote it in the Bible." When Walter leaned close to slip the roll of candy in beside her knitting, his jacket brushed her cheek. "Is it snowing?" she asked. "You smell of snow."

Rocking back on his heels, he shook his head, tucked a strand of hair behind her ear. "Why the hell they couldn't leave your braid . . . heads would roll if Marta was here."

Ilsa pursed her lips to keep from telling him. Why make trouble even though she knows it was Walter's Lydia who told that woman to cut her hair, when all she wanted was a washing. *I heat water from the rain barrel for rinsing our hair. Mine and the two girls. The water from the well is too hard, so much iron that Annaliese's blonde curls are streaked with rust.*

Ilsa's hand tugged at the stiff fan of hair over her ear. "Lydia," she muttered.

"What?" Walter's eyes behind the thick glasses were grey as the winter sky. When did Walter get glasses? *On my side, everyone has good eyes. Only poor little Bruno with his lazy eye needs glasses for school.*

Ilsa shook her head and turned the worn pages of the Bible. *Bruno likes the coloured pictures in the middle. Elijah in his chariot of fire. I imagine myself aboard that chariot, the mane of the white horse streaming against crimson clouds, my best navy dress billowing in the wind, my hand raised in farewell.*

"Mutti?" Walter slid the Bible from her knee and held it with his thumb marking her place. He leaned closer and spoke softly. "Jeannie phoned me this morning. She said you and the new lady don't get along."

Ilsa's glance flew furtively to the other side of the

room. She cupped a hand around his ear. "Old Lady Ridley," she whispered. "From the home place."

Walter looked toward Mrs. Ridley who sat swaying on the edge of her bed, mumbling. He shook his head. "No. Those Ridleys must have passed away years ago."

"It is!" she hissed. "Bernice Ridley. You look at the card at the end of the bed."

"She was called Bernice? I only remember his name. Herbert Ridley, the old son-of-a-bitch." He took one more look at Mrs. Ridley, shook his head again. "I don't think so. And if it were, what does it matter now? They moved away when we were all still kids." Then he paged through the Bible with his stout thumb. "*14 Oktober, 1982. Rolf Freidrich Gartner ist gestorben.*" He wrinkled his nose. "Is that right? I thought '83."

She rubbed her eyes. Who was it wanted to know? One of the nurses? Maybe the woman who sat beside her when the little girls in their brown dresses were singing. Always people asked where she was from, how many children, is there a husband.

Mrs. Ridley had managed to reach across the void between her bed and the table and drag the poinsettia onto her lap. She cradled it in her arms and poked at the dirt. "Dry as a bone," she croaked. "Somebody bring me water! I need water." Just as she toppled sideways, Marcella rushed back into the room. "Bernice! You're squashing that pretty flower." She held up a handful of red petal. "Oh, now look!"

The first summer on the farm at Bruderfeldt, I sowed seeds I brought from the old country and the scarlet tissue paper petals of the poppies danced in the wind. When two months passed without rain, Rolf hauled buckets of wa-

141

ter from the slough to the vegetable patch, and I watched him from the window, him pouring the last of the pails around the poppies. A few days later, before I could harvest the seed, a hailstorm pounded the garden to a pulp and stripped the trees. But only our farm. The hail cut a swath the width of our land. Old Man Ridley had a fine crop of barley in the neighbouring field.

Ilsa shifted in her chair, trying to ease the ache in her bad hip. She'd been dozing again. If only it would stop, this sleep that crept up in the middle of business. What were they talking about, she and Walter? Oh yes. "Mrs. Ridley?" she called. Her neighbour was belted into the wheelchair, still clutching the potted plant. Marcella had left the room, but was not far away, her cheerful voice singing from the room across the hall. "Mrs. Ridley!" Ilsa called again. This time the woman looked up, her eyes a startling forget-me-not blue. "How long is your husband dead?"

The answer seemed to come from far away, but clear as a chime. "Why, he died in '76. Dropped dead in the field. Found by Richard Fyffe, come to help with combining."

Ilsa let her feet drop off the foot rests and walked her chair to the dividing line between the two halves of the room. "What was his name?"

The moment of calm was past, the tremor returning to shake Mrs. Ridley like a faded flower in the wind. Her hands fluttered and tangled in the leaves of the poinsettia. "Go away!" she wailed. "Leave me be! I'm dying!"

"Herbert was his name!" Ilsa shouted. "Herbert Rid-

142

ley, who wouldn't give a thirsty child a pail of water!"
She looked frantically for Walter, to tell him it was so.
She was locked here with Mrs. Herbert Ridley.

*Fourteen days on the ship, all four children sick with
measles and still so weak by the time we docked we were
afraid we'd be kept behind, quarantined. But a kind doctor
from the Red Cross convinced the immigration officer that
we should be allowed to go on to the relatives who awaited
us. Five days on the train, a month crowded into the tiny
home of Rolf's brother and then finally we had our own
land. The well still to be dug, but the Englishman from
whom we bought the farm—leaving after only a month
because his wife and new baby died—told us that the
neighbour, Ridley, welcomed him to draw as much water
as he needed. Just a half mile down the road to his gate,
an easy walk for the children, certainly for the three eldest.
How was the Englishman to know that the gate opened
only for the right names? That Ridley was still fighting the
Battle of the Somme.*

"His name was Herbert Ridley!" Ilsa shouted again.

Mrs. Ridley covered her eyes, shreds of peat soil
clinging to her nails. "I don't know you!"

When Walter and the mean-faced nurse ran into the
room, Ilsa was at the window again, staring into the
dusk.

Supper was ham, mashed potatoes and peas. Mrs. Ridley was not at the same table anymore but parked on
the other side of the dining room. "See?" the afternoon
nurse clucked when she steered Ilsa to her place. "We
had to move poor Bernice because your son made a
fuss. Just when she was starting to talk, and feel at

143

home. Shame on you. You with your lovely family and she with nobody."

Ilsa spooned the last of her rice pudding. Miserable stuff, but she had a sweet tooth, so she ate. She had her own teeth and a good appetite, not like some of these poor people who hung over the plates until someone came to mash a few peas past their lips. On each table was a tiny Christmas tree. Lydia would roast a goose for Christmas Eve, Walter said. Ilsa smacked her lips at the taste of memory. *I will make the prune stuffing. None of the girls, not even Annaliese, can do it right. Lazy little Marta will try to hide in the barn with the kittens. And Walter wanting to go to Lydia's after church instead of coming home to open the presents. That Lydia . . .*

"Ilsa. Ilsa?" Someone was shaking her arm, talking about Lydia. Back in her room now, in the cold chair and the light so dim she could barely make out the shadow calling her name.

"Marcella?" Her voice sounded thick in her own ears.

"No, Marcella went home a long time ago." One of the night girls she didn't know draped an afghan over her knees. "You're so cold you're shaking. I'll be back in a minute and help you to bed. Your daughter-in-law phoned. Lydia. She said she made you an appointment in the morning with the hairdresser. How nice you're going to look with your hair curled for Christmas. And so lucky to spend it with your family."

My sisters all have curls. But my hair is white-blonde, strong and straight as the tail of a horse. Hair down to my hips. Each morning I fix it in a braid as thick as my wrist, then coil and pin it at the nape of my neck. Both Marta

144

and Bruno are dark like Rolf. Walter and Annaliese are fair like me.

She licked her lips. The ham had left her with a terrible thirst, but she hadn't the strength to drag the pitcher from the floor. Fumbling with the paper sleeve, she unwrapped her roll of peppermints and pressed one past her dry lips. The curtain between the beds was drawn.

Ilsa closed her eyes again, the blanket warming her legs, the Christmas lights outside the window bleeding the walls pink, and the taste of the candy sweet and fresh. From down the hall, there was a surge of music and then it grew faint. More Christmas carols, this time from the radio the nurses kept at the desk. Silent night . . . *Heilige Nacht.* She hummed, letting the sound swell in the room.

There was a stirring on the other side of the drape, the smacking click of dentures, a dry swallow, then a rising moan.

"Go to sleep, you mean old woman!" *Alles schläft, einsam wacht* . . . Ilsa's voice was still strong, still a rich soprano.

"I need water! The pails are too heavy to carry. They'll bring on the baby again." Mrs. Ridley wailed like a lost child. "Too soon, too soon!"

"What do you know of babies? You chased my children away with the broom. Like chickens or stray dogs. All they wanted was a few pails of water from your well. Chased them like dogs!" Ilsa sat up and yanked open the drawer in her bedside table. "Four miles they had to walk. Little children. Walter carried Marta on his shoulders the last mile. His hands were raw from the wire on the pail."

"All my babies dead before they were alive." The curtain dividing them billowed as though a wind had entered the room. "And him, the mean old bastard, always stinking of manure and always on me." The voice grew stronger, the room colder. "Wait a few months, the doctor said. Your wife needs to rest. But did he listen?"

Ilsa shuffled through hairpins and handkerchiefs. "Be still! How can I think with this racket going on? *Where is my apron? I need to light the oven for the goose. Walter is coming home and Marta* . . . Be quiet you old woman! Too mean to give children a pail of water!"

"On me every night like an animal!"

"Bernice! Ilsa!" The nurse swept the curtain aside, and stood between the beds. "Let me get you both settled or you'll have everyone else in an uproar." Frowning, she retrieved the water jug from the hiding place and filled their two glasses. She handed Ilsa the paper cup of pills, and the water. Mrs. Ridley had fallen back onto the pillow, her jaw slack. The nurse dumped the tablets into the yawning mouth, sloshed in water, then hoisted the woman to sitting just long enough to watch her swallow.

Within minutes, Ilsa's dress was whisked over her head, the worn nightgown pulled on in its place, one last trip to the toilet and the light was dimmed. She lay breathless under the thin blanket, wishing only that Marta would remember one day to bring the featherbed from the farm. Down the hall the carols played on . . . *Schlaf in himmlischer Ruh', Schlaf in himmlischer Ruh'*. And from the other bed she heard weeping.

"Oh sleep now, Mrs. Ridley," she whispered. "Just sleep."

They must look, Ilsa thought, like bookends the way they sat in their matching chairs. Mrs. Ridley in a fluffy blue robe, her hair brushed into a frizzy halo. Ilsa herself, like a traveller waiting for a bus, with her handbag in her lap, her good black coat bunched around her shoulders. She'd folded a triangle of grey wool over the fussy cap of curls, and knotted it under her chin to form a soft hood. She hoped Lydia would be satisfied when she saw this hair. How stupid she looked.

She was sweating from the extra layer under her best silk dress. She could feel the ribbing on the sweatshirt bunched around her neck. When she lifted her foot onto the metal rest on the wheelchair, a pink cuff peeked out between the hem of her coat and the furry top of her winter boot.

"Good grief, Oma! How long have you been bundled up waiting?" Jeannie breezed into the room, slim and smart in a belted red wool coat.

"Jeannie!" Ilsa felt tears sharp as pinpricks. "Your Mutti, too, always looked so pretty in red."

"Of course she did. She looked pretty in everything." She touched the edge of her grandmother's scarf. "And did you know you look like a wise little owl hiding in there. The Handi-Bus is here, and I got your pills from the nurse."

"When she was a girl, I made her a red coat. She and Bruno both so beautiful, so rosy-cheeked in red."

Jeannie crouched in front of her and gently lifted her

hands. "Oma, please don't start on Bruno. You know Bruno died long ago. Long before I was born."

Ilsa looked into the dark eyes of her granddaughter, eyes just like the two boys. "Of course I know this. I'm his mother. I was talking about his mittens. I knitted him a red scarf and mittens. Stop looking at me so serious." She let her glasses slide down her nose. "I wore the suit you brought me." When she looked down at her coat, she could see that the buttons were wrong. She'd missed the bottom two. This was why one side of the collar caught on her scarf each time she moved her head. She fumbled with stiff fingers.

Jeannie leaned over and began to undo the buttons. "I see that. Did you know that people wear those suits without anything over top?"

Ilsa shook her head. "Not on Christmas Eve."

Jeannie tugged the collar smooth. "The only bad news is that Aunty Annaliese probably won't get here tonight. Big snowstorm in Toronto and the airport's closed, maybe until tomorrow. Bad timing for the holiday travellers."

There was a sigh from Mrs. Ridley's chair.

"Oma," Jeannie whispered. "Isn't Mrs. Ridley going anywhere for Christmas?"

She shook her head again, a finger to her lips. "No family. She lost so many babies. It broke her heart."

Jeannie stared at her. "How do you know that?"

Ilsa flipped her wrist at Mrs. Ridley, struggling with the other hand to help Jeannie with the last button. "She told me."

"SHE told you?"

"Well of course. She tells everything. Talks all day and all night too, you should know by now."

Mrs. Ridley's head drooped. She snored softly.

"See how tired she is. She has to sleep all day because she talks all night."

"I know she talks, Oma, but I didn't think you listened. You told Uncle Walter she's someone you knew from the farm. Why didn't you tell me?"

Ilsa set the brakes on her wheelchair and inched forward on the seat. "Maybe she isn't who I thought." When she rose out of the chair, Jeannie offered an arm, but she leaned on it only a moment before she took the few steps to the window sill. There was still one hidden pitcher, this one tucked days ago behind the drapes. She bore it across the room in both hands, taking steps like a child just learning to walk, breath ragged by the time she reached Mrs. Ridley's bedside table. She set the jug next to the poinsettia, then grasped the edge of the table with one hand, the arm of Mrs. Ridley's chair with the other. Bernice Ridley opened her blue eyes. Ilsa released the hand on the table letting her weight lean on her good hip so that she could stand straight. She felt so tall, so heavy beside this ghost of a woman. Jeannie was behind her now with the wheelchair.

When she felt the gentle nudge of the chair on the back of her knees, she let the girl guide her into the seat. Then she leaned forward, her palm outstretched.

"*Frohe Weihnnachten, Frau Ridley.*"

A thin white hand rose to meet hers. "Merry Christmas, Mrs. Gartner."

149

STORM WARNING

Jess has been staring at the ceiling for hours, possibly all night. But it's only since dawn she's noticed the water stain in the corner above the window. A dark blot that starts on the ceiling and trickles down the flowery wallpaper almost to the floor. She doesn't remember if it was there last summer, or the summer before, or eight years ago when Brian first brought her home to New Brunswick to meet his family. She's always been blind to imperfections in this house. Awestruck by a bedroom that has belonged to a boy for his whole life, and a family whose greatest sorrow is that the eldest son has moved away from home.

Brian stirs and she shifts onto her side so that they're still touching. She can never sleep without the feel of his skin. She pillows her head next to his and whispers in his ear, "There's a water stain. Does the roof leak?"

As always, he's instantly awake. Eyes wide, he turns his head. "Of course. This is the stormy side of the house." He plays with Jess's thick black hair, arranging strands across the snowy pillowcase. She could purr when he does this, every nerve in her scalp dancing with his fingers. She wishes they could hide in this room for the whole week.

"I'm taking the boat out," Brian says, "I don't suppose you'd come along?"

She shakes her head. He keeps hoping she'll be reborn a sailor. Jess catches his hand where his fingers are traveling the curve of her throat. "Do you mind that it'll be a whole year before you can come home again?" she asks.

"If I was that much a mommy's boy, I'd never have left in the first place. And I wouldn't have found you." His other hand bends her elbow to work her arm free of the sleeve. "Mom always told everyone I was smarter than I looked."

But later, in the kitchen, Jess feels awkward as ever when she opens three cupboard doors before she finds the coffee mugs. When the first thing her mother-in-law tells Brian as he comes through the door is that Priscilla called. As though it's the most natural thing in the world for an old girlfriend to phone before breakfast. But like Brian's mom, Priscilla has probably been up for hours. There's bread dough rising on the counter, fresh scones for breakfast.

"Let me do the dishes," Jess says.

"Then what would I do? You two go on out and have fun."

Behind the good-natured smile, Jess recognizes her mother-in-law's discomfort at the prospect of spending a half hour alone with her. They have never been able to convince Brian's parents to visit them in Edmonton. There at least they would see Jess in her own kitchen, her own home. She can bake muffins, brew up a decent pot of tea, but feels, each time she crosses the threshold of this house, that she's kicked her domesticity off like ill-fitting shoes and left it outside the door.

The women in Brian's family are fair and round with a placid good nature, a fecundity in keeping with his father's herd of Guernseys. Jess has a storm cloud of black hair and eyes that flash like lightning bolts. Long ago, a social worker described Jess and her brother, Louis, as "wild little animals". Jess has never been able to pull that sliver from the thin skin of her childhood memory.

She knows she is a puzzle to Brian's mom. She's overheard Marie say to Brian's dad, "Never met anyone who seemed so much from away. Have you?"

When she slips her plate and cup into the soapy water, and is shooed away, Jess waits on the front porch, watching the voracious traffic of bees in the lupins until Brian comes bounding away from the phone and out the door.

"What'll you do all morning?" he asks.

Avoid your mother, she wants to say, but instead, "I have a book. I'll sit in the sun and read."

He frowns at a bank of clouds on the horizon. "Maybe not for long. Not in the sun anyway."

"Is it going to storm, do you think?" She struggles to keep panic from her voice.

"Nah!" He plants a kiss on her forehead, then lopes toward the truck. "Just some good wind coming in!"

She can't stifle, "Be careful!"

He tosses it away with a laughing, "Trust me!"

Jess watches the truck drop out of sight beyond the first hill. Her father-in-law appears around the corner of the barn with a pitchfork in one hand, raises the other in greeting, but trudges on into the pasture without stopping to talk. Brian warned her eight years ago when he brought her home for the first time, that Charlie spends his words with the economy of a Trappist monk. But in spite of, or maybe because of his reserve, he is the one with whom Jess feels easiest.

Jess climbs the stairs to the bedroom for her book, but instead of going down again, she sits in a chair beside the window watching the road. Like a fisherman's wife, she thinks, watching for the sea to return her man. Finally she picks up the novel Brian's sister lent her yesterday, but she knows she won't finish it. Louanne says she loves a book that's good for a cry. Already Jess can taste the sad ending, and she's losing her appetite. She's been reading a while when the curtains begin to billow against her knees and the room is plunged into gloom. The heavy deck of cloud is overhead, pulling the wind with it. Down in the yard, Charlie is closing the barn door. With his hand over his eyes, he scans the sky.

Jess grabs Brian's jacket from the back of the chair, tears down the stairs. Brian has taken the truck, but she knows the way across the fields. No more than a fifteen minute walk, ten at a run.

Always, when she smells a storm, Jess's heart races and she's whirled into the eye of the tornado. She was driving cab on the south edge of Edmonton the day piles of coal black clouds rolled toward the city, bulging and heaving, gathering an eerie jaundiced light. When the car began to buck in the rising wind, Jess turned it around, driving furiously toward the edge of the storm. She hesitated when she saw a man at the side of the road braced against a mileage sign, his hair, his jacket, the legs of his jeans plastered to him. A glance at the sky in the rearview mirror and her foot hit the brake. She pulled onto the shoulder, backed to where he was standing and flung open the passenger door. Both man and door were almost ripped away by the wind before he pulled himself gasping into the car and heaved the door shut.

Jess put her foot to the floor, instinctively heading for home. They were silent except for Brian's ragged breath until a tight black funnel came spiraling out of the clouds.

"Jaysus! Is that what I think it is?" His voice was muffled in the thick heat.

Brian's family loves to tell the story of how Jess saved him, but it's the story of his defection that she's heard a dozen times. His mother and sister blame Priscilla, his childhood sweetheart, for his leaving. Even nine years later, with Priscilla trailing three babies in her wake, they say she scared him off, pulled too hard when what he needed was a little slack.

When Brian went west to look for work, he promised Priscilla he'd be back in six months. She gave him six months' grace. After the year, she called his bluff and married his cousin. On the day Priscilla, veiled in white, lifted her face to Ralph's broad, freckled smile, the tornado cut a swath through Edmonton and, but for Jess, would have sucked Brian into its eye and blown him clear back home to Moncton.

154

To Jess, all of this is ancient history. She dumped her own past when she turned eighteen and was given an indifferent farewell from her last foster home. Brian's mother presses her for memories of her people, her "real kin" she calls them.

"I don't remember." Jess's voice falls flat when she's forced to talk about her family.

"But surely you remember something, darlin'. You were eight years old when they took you away."

"I don't remember."

Jess can't blame Marie for being curious. Can't blame the wariness she sees in her mother-in-law's eyes. Her grandchildren, after all, will be heir to the mystery. This summer though, the conversation stays deliberately away from babies, at least in Marie's kitchen.

On their first day back, when Jess and Brian met Priscilla on the street with her new baby in a sling, Brianna flushed and sleepy in her stroller, and Ralphine skipping ahead, the first thing Priscilla said: "Well, hey, you two. Still no babies?"

Brian's hand reached out to touch the baby's cheek but he kept the other linked with Jess's. "Aw Priscilla, you're making up for all the rest of us. Keeps you too busy to get in trouble, I bet." He gave Jess's hand a squeeze. "Can you believe this girl? She's landlocked. She used to sneak away from helping her mom and sail with anyone who'd take her out."

"If you weren't family, Brian Maguire, I'd punch you for that. What a thing to say! Jess will think I was some kind of tramp."

The scope of Brian's kinship astounds Jess. Cousins, aunts, uncles orbit the farm in an infinite galaxy. She

155

and her brothers and sisters were more like a meteor shower, almost all of them burning out before they fell to earth in adulthood.

Every day while Brian and Jess are home at the farm, someone drops in to visit and share a meal. Last night, when Jess brought the cups from the living room, she caught Priscilla and Brian's sister, Louanne, gossiping at the kitchen sink, their backs to the door. Priscilla, as always, was wearing the azure green that matches her eyes; a soft sweater hugging her abundant breasts and a green satin ribbon securing the plait of blonde hair.

"I've heard that sometimes," she said in a low murmur, "the partners aren't compatible. It's like the woman's egg is hostile to the man's sperm. But when people like that split up and find new partners, they'll both be fertile."

Jess stepped back into the hallway, eased the door closed with her foot, leaned against the wall, her cheek hot on the plaster. In the living room, the men were haranguing about bringing back capital punishment. A local girl had been murdered this spring. While Jess was still in the room, Brian had tried to change the subject. His dad was dozing in his chair. When Jess reached down to pick up Charlie's cup, the corner of his mouth quirked up in a smile and he winked. Jess suspects that Brian has told Charlie about her brother. Brian's mom and sister know that Jess is one of nine kids divided out to half a dozen foster homes, but they don't know that Louis, the brother just a year older than she, the one with whom she moved from home to home, is serving a life sentence for killing his best friend.

Crimes of passion, they're called, so Jess has heard.

156

Louis gone berserk because he thought he finally had someone who loved him, and she was screwing around with his best friend. Still, Jess wanted to scream on his behalf, he only went after the friend. He kept right on loving the girl. Louis, who'd never loved or been loved by anyone but her.

Caught there between infertility in the kitchen, and punishment by death in the parlor, Jess stacked the cups on the floor in the hallway, and chose a third door. She tiptoed into the bedroom where Priscilla and Louanne had nested their babies among coats and pillows on the bed and settled on a corner of the chenille spread, her finger reaching out to stroke a buttery little cheek.

He looks like Brian, this wee nephew. Jess has seen the baby pictures, the school pictures, the graduation and wedding pictures. Marie's albums are a chronicle of family life.

Jess's chronicle is a plastic folder of wallet-sized school pictures that starts when she was seven and finishes in high school. Grades five, eight and eleven are missing for reasons she can't remember. She missed the picture day? She moved to another foster home before the pictures came back? Someone forgot to send the money? Neither she nor Brian are camera buffs, so their marriage is compressed into a handful of pictures taken at their wedding, and her formal convocation portrait which Brian proudly mounted on the living room wall. That, everyone smugly assures them, will change with kids.

When they'd just begun trying to make a baby, they'd stay awake in the dark talking about names, about bringing their child home to the family. He'd teach their kids to sail, Brian said. On their first summer home to Moncton, Jess was game to share Brian's love of sailing. He patiently walked her through the "rigging," the "launching," the jargon as light on her tongue as salt spray. They'd been sailing clear for almost an hour before she gave thought to the ocean floor.

"How deep is the water here, do you think?"

"Well, if you're considering diving over and going down for a look you'll need to pack a lunch for the trip."

"Seriously, Brian, how deep?"

"Seriously, Jess, it's so deep it's irrelevant."

She'd peered into opaque green glass, then up into endless sky, and was overcome with a whirling panic. Dizzy beyond reason, she jerked back, the boat tipped and she was dumped, flailing in the icy water.

When they were finally back on land again, she sprawled in the wet sand with Brian's arms anchoring her in place. "Oh God, I've never been so scared in all my life. I'm sorry."

"It's okay. I never wanted to sleep with a sailor. And I've been waiting for my turn to save you."

The day Jess rescued Brian, they'd hardly spoken as she steered the cab through wildly buffeting wind. When the windshield wipers surrendered to the deluge, she parked, and let the car idle. "Guess we'd better wait it out." For the first time, she looked closely at the man beside her. His wet hair had dried into a deep wave across his forehead, his cheeks had lost their pallor and gleamed with the sun-burnished health of a young labourer, and he sat loose and easy. But it was his eyes that were Jess's undoing—intensely blue with circles of turquoise around the iris that sent a jolt of electricity straight through her like lightning to the base of a tree. She turned away to hide the flush in her cheeks, and stared into the rain. "That was a pretty stupid place to be hitching, you know."

"Yeah? Well, I don't have a car and I was gettin' out to a job. And pickin' up hitchhikers is pretty stupid too."

"Yeah? Well, I'm a cabbie. Picking up people is what I do. Would you rather I'd left you there? We can go back if you want."

"No," he said. "I think this was meant to be."

She'd found what she was looking for in his calm face, and when the rain slowed she drove the few blocks to her basement apartment. They stumbled inside, and into each other's arms.

Later, when the storm had passed, Brian looked at her with a stricken face. "How did you know I wasn't a danger to you? You could be killed bringing a complete stranger home like this."

She shrugged. "I just knew. And I was right, wasn't I? You said it was meant to be."

He'd stared at her long and hard, and she was afraid that he'd find enough to send him away. Know that this wasn't the first time she'd taken a stranger home. But it would be the last.

They went back the next day to the spot where Brian had been standing. There was no sign of the mileage post, and a mountain of rubble stood on the other side of the highway where there'd been a warehouse. Gulls circled in a cloudless sky.

Two months later, they were married in a quick civil

ceremony with Brian's foreman and his wife as their witnesses. Jess drove cab for the three years it took Brian to earn his electrician's papers, then he bullied her into registering at the University of Alberta.

"You want to drive a taxi for the rest of your life?" They were in bed on a Sunday morning, and likely to stay there until afternoon.

"Of course not, but now that you're working I thought I'd look around for something else. And who knows, maybe one of these days I'll get pregnant."

"I've been thinking we might be trying too hard, you know. People always say that if you want to have a kid, just take out a big mortgage or plan something that'll take up the next five years of your life, and that'll do it. Jess, you're the smartest person I know. You said yourself you never did a bit of work in school, and you breezed through. Here's a chance to kick back and get what you deserve. If you get pregnant, all the better. You can take night classes and I'll look after the baby."

There'd been no need for night classes. She earned her Education degree in three years, taking winter, spring and summer sessions with just a quick break for the trip to New Brunswick at the end of each summer.

She's been teaching high school math for four years now, hoping at the beginning of every term that she won't be there for the end. It looks as though she'll stay forever. Come back here to the farm each summer with empty arms, and Brian will have to settle for teaching his nephew to sail. Or Priscilla's three.

All this storm of memory, of what's yet to be, pounds through Jess's head as she flies across Charlie's pasture, and then the neighbour's, and finally scrambles down the last rocky slope. When she arrives gasping on the dunes, there are gulls pitching like sailboats on the black ceiling of cloud. A dog runs pell mell along the beach, yelping at the waves. With her face pulled deep into the collar of the blue nylon windbreaker, Brian's musky smell ripples around her.

Suddenly, Jess's gaze captures a triangle of white. She fumbles in the jacket pocket for Brian's binoculars, but behind the lenses, she loses the boat. Her long scrutiny of the rise and fall of the waves leaves her queasy. She closes her eyes, breathes deeply and feels her heart begin to calm.

When she looks out at the sea again, she stares hard at the patch of white and digs her heels into the sand, bracing against the wind.

She welcomes the intrusion of Charlie's voice when he tramps across the dunes toward her. "Did you find him? You should have waited. I'd have driven you. You didn't hear me calling after you?"

She's never heard him speak so many sentences at once. She points, but for a moment a swirl of mist obliterates even the shoreline. "He's out there. I think . . . I hope it's him."

Charlie's breathing hard, and fumbles in his pocket for cigarettes. It's just six months since Brian quit smoking, Jess trying hard not to nag. The corners of Charlie's mouth turn up at her stern expression. "Oh, now don't you be giving me grief about the weeds. I get enough from the rest of them." His forehead wrinkles.

"Don't look so worried, Jess, he's coming in. The boy's had lots of practice with storms."

"But he pushes his luck. I know he makes a joke of it, and I know someone else would have picked him up, but when I met him he was standing smack dab in the path of a tornado." The splash of white is visible again. She raises the glasses to her eyes, then lowers them quickly. "It's him. I can see the red stripes on his shirt." She tries to blink away what this time is unmistakable—a flash of emerald green beside the red—and glances at Charlie who is watching the progress of the boat impassively, smoke curling around the brim of his sweat-stained cap. "Do you ever sail, Charlie?" she asks, trying to fill the silence.

He purses his lips, the cigarette clamped and bobbing in one corner. "Nah."

"You don't fish either, do you?"

"Nope."

"Or swim?"

"Christ, no."

"Why? You've lived a stone's throw from the bay all your life."

"I'm a farmer. Don't like the water. Like you, I guess."

"Me?" She begins to methodically snap the metal buttons on the jacket. "I'm scared to death of the ocean."

"That's because you're not used to it. Guess we're all scared of what we don't know." He grinds the cigarette butt into the coarse sand with the heel of his boot.

She takes a deep breath, tastes the salt in her lungs.

"Did you know my brother killed someone?" He nods. "Did Brian tell anyone else?"

"Nope."

"Charlie?" She feels a stinging on the backs of her eyes where the tangy breeze could not have touched. "Do you think I'll ever really fit into this family?"

He takes a quick step toward her and, in an awkward stiff-armed motion, circles her shoulder to pull her face against the coarse flannel of his shirt. Then, as abruptly, he releases her. "Aw, Jess, you're ours, just like Brian and Louanne."

With the memory of the old man's chest still warm on her face, she squints at the horizon, then reaches for his hand. Between her own smooth palms, it feels as coarse and dry as the ridges of sand under her feet. "Louis's all I've got for family. I haven't seen the rest of them in almost twenty years. And what Brian has here just blows me away. Sometimes I feel like I'm from another planet."

"Well, I guess family is like ocean. If you're not used to it, it scares you." He holds out his hand for the binoculars. She hesitates, tracing a circle in the sand with her toe before she relinquishes the glasses. While he scans the sea, focuses and watches the bobbing sail, she rams her hands into the deep pockets, fingers the handful of change Brian always carries, and bites her lip.

When Charlie lowers the binoculars, he loops the strap around his neck and lets them dangle against his suspenders. He hands her a ring of keys. "Here now, it's a long walk back and the rain's coming any minute. You take my car and I'll wait and come back with Brian in the truck."

163

"I can handle a bit of rain. I'll wait." She sets her jaw, fixes her eyes on the sea.

"Serves no purpose. You pulled him out of one storm, but he wouldn't want you doing it twice. Now you go on, and tell Marie we'll be wet and wanting tea."

"Could you see him?"

"Yup." He looks away from her, his eyes intent on the boat.

Even without the glasses she can see that the ocean has begun to roll, whitecaps foaming around the pitching sail. The wind plasters Charlie's wide khaki pants to his legs. "It's picking up. Are you sure he's coming in?"

"Yup."

"Well, then I guess I'll let you bring him safely home." She catches her writhing hair and tucks it into the collar of the jacket. "Charlie," she says "you don't have to tell him I was here." When he nods, she turns to leave.

"Jess?" She stops a few feet away. "That brother of yours, the one who made the bad choice. Do you love him less now than you did before?"

He's like a rock, his solid presence standing between her and the sea. "No," she says, "I have to love him more."

On the walk back to the car, the wind flattens Brian's jacket to Jess like a second skin.

TRESPASSES

Sylvia slams the window so hard the glass ripples. Aftershock reverberates through her shoulders, but her neighbour doesn't look up. Deafened by his weed eater, he's sculpting a fussy property line. Every *tziiiitt* means Walter has felled another clump of lily-of-the-valley. Sylvia grips the edge of the desk. Without that mooring, she'd sail out the door, rip the weed whacker out of his hands and use it to carve her initials in the perfect helmet of his hair.

Finally, there's blessed silence. Closing her eyes, she releases the pen. Lets go of the swirl of platitudes in her head and welcomes the thick absence of sound and thought.

She'd make a pot of tea and take her cup into the sunshine, but years of living next to door to Walter and Doris have etched their garden routine on her brain. Surely as thunder follows lightning, the Toro will charge across the lawn now that the edging is done.

She dares a peek, slides the streaky pane of glass along a gritty track. Really, she needs to spring-clean —dust blinds, polish windows, slap stain on the fence —but each time she approaches the jobs she and Steve did together for thirty-nine years, her ears strain to hear his tuneless humming. The small of her back aches for his hand when she lifts the bucket of soapy water he would have carried.

The screen is redolent with dust. Next door, the windows gleam and Sylvia imagines Doris with spray bottle and cloth in hand.

Tomorrow. Today, the thank you notes are three months overdue.

For your kindness and support while Steven was ill . . . the same numb thank you over and over, but for family members, extra assurance that life goes on. *You were right when you said I would feel as though there's a stone in my chest. I think the back of my throat has turned to granite. But the weather's fine here now. Tomorrow, I'll tackle the perennial beds.*

A line through her sister-in-law's name on the list, one more envelope sealed and stamped, and then the lawnmower fades to the back.

While the kettle boils, Sylvia leans on the counter and eats cottage cheese from the plastic tub. Why dirty one plate, pull one chair askew from the table? She pours directly into a cup, jerking the string on the teabag until the water is amber and fragrant with bergamot.

Steaming tea in hand, she soaks up sun on the front step, face tilted to the warmth, bare feet curled against cold cement. When the cup is empty, she wanders onto

166

the grass, stopping short of the property line. Her toes fit neatly into the lush green scallops where Walt's fertilizer has leached into her lawn.

"Sylvia!" Tall and gaunt in his beltless grey coveralls, Walt curls over her like a plume of smoke. "We need to talk about the trailer."

Sylvia glances over her shoulder at the unfenced strip of property between their houses. The utility trailer that Walt and Steve went halves on years ago sits on a patch of gravel straddling the two yards. It hasn't been used since the last time Steve hauled manure. As always, Walt staged a production worthy of an Oscar, hosing, and muttering, even though Steve left the trailer as clean as he'd found it. Sylvia had fumed."If you don't go over there and give him a piece of your mind, I will."

Steve's blue eyes peered over his newspaper. "Syl, please. That's like pouring kerosene on fire. Just ignore him. We've been neighbours all these years and we'll be neighbours for many more."

Sylvia draws a deep breath, trying to invoke the spring fragrance of horse manure. A light broadcasting over the rose beds inspired Steve's crimson Europeana to produce blooms as big as soup bowls.

When he stops picking at spruce galls on the lowest branches of her tree, Walt squints into the tower of green. "Must be dark as a tomb in there with this thing blocking your bedroom window." When she doesn't answer, lost still in memories of roses, he advances a step. "I warned Steve twenty years ago he was planting too near the house."

"What do you want?" She slides between Walter and the tree, forcing him back onto his own property, so

167

close she can smell coffee on his breath. He's on his break, the quiet just an interlude. "About the trailer? What do you want to know?"

"Can I sell it? I'll clean up that corner with some sod."

Sylvia's head shakes as soon as she hears "sell". Every time the kids come over, someone drags out "sell".

"No." She rattles calendar leaves in her mind. This must be May. Time for a trip to the mushroom farm. "The garden needs a load of manure."

Sylvia knows that a year ago, before Steve died, before everyone began handling her with velvet gloves, Walt would have snorted and told her what her garden needed was a good dose of Roundup.

"Aw Syl," he rolls the words around his mouth. "Just hire someone to look after the yard."

Like hell she will. She can't bear the thought of trespassers in the garden, even though she promised Steve she'd stay away from the power tools.

"Please be sensible when I'm gone," he'd said, his hands on her shoulders. His touch, by then, had all the weight of a shadow. "I keep imagining you cutting grass in your bare feet."

She promised to leave the power mower in the garage and use the push mower. She loves the clackety-clack and the spray of green confetti on her toes. She also promised she'd look after his roses.

"I'm taking the trailer out next weekend. My half stays, Walt. Do what you want with yours."

Sylvia turns so quickly she staggers in a whirl of vertigo. Shrugging away the steadying arm Walt offers, she plods back to the house. Inside, she drags out the phone book and calls the mushroom farm. She's just in time. Today, tomorrow and Sunday there's an "all you can load" special at the manure pile.

Next she phones David. "Could you stop by on your way home from work tomorrow and help me hitch up the trailer? I'm going to the mushroom farm."

"Mom!" There's gentle exasperation in his voice. "Why?"

"Because it's time." She leans on the kitchen counter, staring out at the crabapple all a-flounce with white.

"Why don't you ask Walter to share a load? I'm sure he'd pick it up."

"Walter doesn't use manure in his garden. He's been whining about the stink from ours for years."

"Try him anyway. I have to work tomorrow. Last time I was over he caught me on the way to the car and said he wants to help. He said he offered to fertilize the lawn and you told him to get lost."

"I never. I told him if I need his help I know where to find him." Through the kitchen window, she can see Walt sweeping cobwebs off the eaves of his garage.

A robin lands on a branch of the crabapple, a bit of red string dangling from its beak, and dives into the centre of the tree. "Oh, David! The robin's back." The sight of that cheerful bird sends tears tracking the grooves from Sylvia's cheeks to her mouth.

"Let Walter help, Mom. He's a good neighbour."

"Of course he is, but he's irritating, and he's . . ." She tastes salt at the corner of her lips and dabs at her eyes with a tea towel. "Never mind, David. I'll think of something."

Her hand is too shaky to finish the cards, and she's

169

run out of words. Sylvia tucks her hair under Steve's sweat-stained baseball cap, and digs a pair of gumboots out of the closet. She clomps out to the trailer and contemplates the hitch, running her palm over ridges of rust, trying to remember how Steve's hands married metal to metal.

The car is backed onto the gravel, the metal tongue on the trailer licking the hitch when Walt looms up out of a clump of juniper. "Sylvia, what the hell are you doing?"

"Good God! Don't sneak around like that." One hand on her throat, she steadies herself on the trailer with the other. "Is it your hearing or your memory that's failing you? I told you I'm going for manure."

Three long strides bring him so close she's trapped against the trailer. Then he gets a cagey look, a little twitching around the lips and tightening of eyes. "The hitch is broken. See." He steps forward and rattles a dangling link of chain. "Safety's gone."

Sylvia leans in, hauls down on the latch with both hands and the hitch locks over the ball. Two side steps, a dash to the car door, key in the ignition and she's spinning gravel. "It'll be fine," she shouts through the open window.

For the first ten minutes of the drive, she sucks on the four broken nails on her left hand. The drive is longer than she remembers, but the wait at the manure pile is short. This late in the day, the serious gardeners have come and gone. Sylvia's the last in line and after the backhoe dumps a pungent load into her trailer, she rolls away, and the iron gate clangs shut behind her.

All the way home, she keeps one eye through the rearview mirror on the swaying deck of the trailer. When she cranks the window closed to shut out the jangle of the broken chain, the car smells faintly of Players even though it's three years since Steve quit smoking. *Yeah, yeah,* she mutters, *I know. Be sensible. I'm trying, sweetheart. Honest, I am.*

No sign of Walt when she maneuvers the trailer onto the front lawn, nor through the long hour of flinging manure. Eyes stinging, throat raw from the stench, Sylvia scrapes the last lumps from the trailer, then jumps down and with the back of the shovel pounds a flat face onto the pile where it rides the edge of Walter's lawn.

As though he's been waiting the four hours since she left, Walt is framed in his open garage door with the hose when she drives around back. His lips are pressed in a purple line. "Leave it in the alley!" he barks. "Or I'll wash the shit onto your side of the yard."

Sylvia pulls in close to the fence. The car can stay out until tomorrow, and the mountain of manure can grace the front lawn until David has time to help her spread it. For all she cares, Walt can set fire to the trailer. Still, she gives him a jaunty salute before she sprints to the back door. Then she kicks off the stinking boots, sinks onto the steps in the back entry, and rests her head against the wall until she has the strength to run a hot bath.

After a long soak in the tub, and an hour dozing in front of the television, she falls into bed and instantly into sleep. But at 1:30 Sylvia's eyes fly open.

All those years of nudging Steve, growling at him to roll over, turn off the buzz-saw, and now that she has silence she suffers more than ever from sleeplessness.

171

Tiny frantic insects scratch and crawl under her skin. Red-eyed mice race in the wire cages of her mind. She tosses and turns and finally pads down the hall in her nightgown.

A full moon hangs in the kitchen window. The refrigerator light is all she needs to pour a cup of milk, warm it in the microwave and drag a chair into the puddle of moonbeams in the middle of the floor. When the cup is rinsed and set on the drainboard to dry, Sylvia leans into the window, face pressed to the screen. But she wants to feel the night like velvet on her cheek, and moves impulsively to the back door.

Barefoot on the cool grass, she can see a faint light in the kitchen window next door. Like Sylvia just minutes before, Doris stands in front of the refrigerator. When she turns, holding the milk carton, Sylvia's hand lifts in an involuntary wave, but she's relieved that Doris doesn't respond. In the turning, Sylvia sees that Doris is naked in her kitchen.

Before Sylvia can tactfully turn her attention to the moon, Walt slides pale and tall into the tableau. Two of them, naked in the night padding together down the hall to share a glass of milk.

Sylvia closes her eyes, but can still see how Doris's shoulders will lift when she feels Walt behind her, how she will lean ever so slightly forward to fit his body to the curves of her own. How the man will cup his wife's breasts with warm, sure hands, encircle her. How he will reach into the back of the cupboard for the bottle of rye, add a generous splash to the warm milk, and hold the cup for her to sip. *Night cap,* he'll say, his hand sliding from her cheek down the slope of her neck, her

172

back, and coming to rest on a pillowy buttock. And then he'll pull her close.

In the silent moonlit movie Sylvia watches on the dark screen of her eyelids, the wife lifts her face for the familiar taste of her husband's lips, then takes his hand and leads him back to bed.

When Sylvia opens her eyes, Doris and Walt's kitchen window is dark. Thankfully, a cloud has scudded across the moon. Doris would be mortified if she knew her neighbour was spying from under the ceiling of crabapple blossom. And what about Walt?

"The old fool," Sylvia whispers. But that isn't it. As she tried to tell David, the problem with Walt is that he's . . . alive.

And so is Sylvia. She knows this because she feels blades of grass sharp between her toes, catches a whiff of manure on the wind, tastes apple scent on the back of her throat, and hears the heavy thud of heartbeat against her breastbone.

THE CAT CAME BACK

Mel trucked Louise's hot meals over to his pal, Larry, for a whole month after Fran died. When Larry protested, Mel held up his hand. "I know. You don't want anybody fussing over you. But Louise sees this as a last favour to Fran. Humour her," he said, "and you'll make my life easier."

What he didn't say was that Louise was raging about the unfairness of Fran's sudden death. She seemed to think Larry had cheated by out-living the good woman who'd cared for him through two heart attacks and a triple by-pass. Still, Louise was a good woman too, and she was determined to keep an eye on Larry, just as she knew Fran would have looked in on Mel had their fortunes been reversed.

Louise's attention was suddenly diverted, though, when her sister in Vancouver had a stroke. "Good thing we both have vacation time," she told Mel. "I have a feeling this will be more than a weekend visit." She'd made plane reservations and had the old brown Samsonite out on the bed.

Mel could think of a hundred places he'd rather spend his holiday than installing bars beside his sister-in-law's toilet. "Y'know," he said, "we could both retire next year and we'd be on permanent weekends. Heck, you could quit now and stay out at the coast as long as Marge needs you."

Louise looked up from the shirt she was folding. "Mel, retirement is one of life's bad jokes. Don't we know at least three people who died within a year of quitting work? And then there's Larry."

She had a point. In the weeks he'd been dropping off the dinners, Mel had mourned the loss of the old Larry as much as he'd mourned Fran's passing. All the early years Mel had envied Larry's carefree bachelorhood were erased by the sad-sack image of his sick and grieving friend. Mel could've pointed out that Larry retired after the bypass surgery, not before. This retirement debate had started six months ago when two guys in Mel's office took buy-outs. He knew that all he had to do was say the word and an envelope would be on his desk. The only thing holding him back was Louise's prediction. She had an irritating way of nailing the grim truth.

Louise snapped the suitcase shut and heaved it off the bed. "There's a pot of chili on the stove. We'll drop it off at Larry's on our way out."

That was two weeks ago. Mel had hoped Louise would forget about feeding Larry after they were back, but tonight, as soon as he put down his fork, she shoved a foil-covered dish across the table.

175

He'd tried to call Larry several times, but the phone had been busy. When he pulled up in front of the bungalow, he was relieved to see the flickering ghost of television through the window. He stepped from the truck, plate in hand, and grimaced. Time to get his stiff knees back to the weight room and sauna.

There must have been a thaw while they were away, because the sidewalk was a sheet of black ice. Mel slid the last few feet and caught the railing just in time to save himself from an ass-over-tea-kettle. The plate slammed against the step, the cover flew off, and the chicken breast skidded over an icy crust of snow. Mel retrieved the meat and re-crimped the foil before the door opened.

Larry looked as though he hadn't left the house in weeks. Green plaid pyjama bottoms pouched around his knees, and his Edmonton Oilers sweatshirt gave off a strong whiff of sweat when he stepped aside to let Mel in.

"You're back! Why'nt you call? Hey, come on in."

Mel held out the plate. "Your phone's been ringing busy." He followed Larry to the kitchen, stepping around a cereal bowl in the middle of the floor.

Larry turned from the fridge where he was rearranging jars to make room for the chicken dinner. "I'm gonna save this one. I ordered Chinese tonight." He pulled a couple of bottles of Big Rock off the top shelf and handed one to Mel.

In the living room, the La-Z-Boy was pulled in close to the television. A glass-topped coffee table, usually aligned with the sofa, sat alongside the recliner like a buffet sidecar. There were pizza boxes stacked under

176

the table and coffee mugs on the floor beside the chair. Cartons of food and a serviette full of bones clustered at one end of the table. Newspapers and bottles littered the other end.

Mel moved a pile of clothes, and sank onto the middle of the sofa. He shook his head when Larry motioned to the cardboard containers. "Ate already."

The clothes beside him looked fresh from the dryer. A knitted afghan hung from the back of Larry's chair, and a sweater or scarf of some kind of ratty-looking black wool was crammed into the corner of the seat. When the black garment began to writhe, the hair on the back of Mel's neck sprang to attention. "What the hell is that!" Yellow sparks flashed from the pile of wool.

"Hey, Earl's back!" Larry scooped up the black lump. He lit up like a kid who's just spied skates under the Christmas tree. "Nine, ten days ago—the night we had the freezing rain—I'm watching the hockey game and I hear this scratching on the front door. Couldn't be, I tell myself. I'm dreaming again." His face went slack. "You know I hate falling asleep, because I keep dreaming about Franny and then I wake up . . ." He turned away, but the saffron eyes of the cat stayed fixed on Mel.

Even though the ears were now chewed-off stumps, there was no mistaking the belligerent pug face of Larry's cat, Earl. Mel shook his head. "I thought Earl croaked," he said.

"Me too. He's been MIA for two years." Larry stroked the cat's head, running his hand over matted fur to a tail warped to a sixty degree angle and hairless from

177

the bend to the tip. "Since I went to Winnipeg for my brother's funeral. Fran let him out the night I left, and he didn't come back." He frowned. "We had a hell of a row over that."

Mel remembered the row. Fran had come to their house sobbing that Larry had accused her of killing Earl. She said she'd made a terrible mistake, marrying a man who loved his cat more than he loved her. That was the year Larry had the first heart attack, and turned into a senior citizen overnight.

Mel took a swig of his beer. "Where do you figure the old guy's been so long?"

"I dunno, but when I opened the door, he streaked for the fridge like he'd only been gone since breakfast." He fondled Earl's mutilated ears. "Didn't think I'd ever fill him up. Don't tell Lou, but Earl finished off that pot of chili."

Mel shuddered. Earl's flatulence was legendary in Larry's bachelorhood when the cat could clear a smoke-filled kitchen in the middle of a poker game. That Fran had agreed to live with a nasty, malodorous cat amazed Larry's pals. Ten years ago, Earl had looked like the next back-alley brawl would be his last. Fran probably assumed he'd be gone from her immaculate house within months. And here he was, resurrected and resting sphinx-like on Larry's knee.

The cat dropped to the floor and wove a crooked path to the hallway. This was another story for Louise's repertoire of life's bad jokes. Not only had Fran failed to outlive Larry, but she'd lost the race to Earl as well. Fortunately, Fran would never know.

There was a thunk from the kitchen. "He's on the

kitchen table. Jumps up there and knocks the phone off the hook. Used to drive Franny nuts." Larry draped the afghan over his legs. "Cold in here." He rubbed his arms. "You want me to turn up the heat?"

Mel shook his head. "I'm good," he said. Christ Almighty, Larry looked like an old man.

"How's Margie?"

Mel had almost forgotten that Larry and Louise's sister were once a hot item. What a pair they'd be now. Larry with his clunker of a heart, and Marge crying all day because the words coming out of the twisted side of her mouth didn't match the ones her brain was screaming. Larry didn't need any more sad stories. "Pretty good. A couple of months and she'll be dancing again."

"Good for her. Me, I'm going on a holiday."

Mel set the bottle down too quickly on the coffee table and winced at the crack of glass on glass. "You're kidding."

Larry shrugged. "What's to kid about? We've gone to Vegas every February for ten years. I was going to take off last week, but then Earl showed up. I couldn't walk out on him after he's been sleeping rough for two years." He leaned forward and put his elbows on his knees. "I still think she did it, you know. The day before I left she said she was calling a fumigator to get rid of the smell of cat piss in the basement, and Earl was going to have to sleep in the garage. I told her we'd talk about it when I got back—hell, I was getting sick of the stench myself—but I figure she decided to take things into her own hands and locked him out." He fished a sparerib out of one of the cardboard containers. "Poor

179

old bugger probably thought I was gone for good and decided to hit the road." He gnawed the length of the bone and added it to the pile on the table.

"You're going to Vegas?"

Earl reappeared at the door to the living room and began the wobbly journey to Larry's chair. He crouched there, shoulders and hips twitching, eyes fixed on the footrest, but couldn't seem to gather the strength for the jump. Larry reached down and lifted the cat to his lap. "That's the plan."

"What about Earl?"

"I was hoping you'd drop in once a day to feed him. Earl always liked you, Mel."

The only sound was the faint beep of the phone from the kitchen. Mel's daughter and son-in-law and the three kids were coming next weekend, and the prospect of a few quiet hours in front of Larry's television wasn't too bad at all. He imagined himself in Larry's chair with the warm weight of the cat on his thighs.

"You think you're up to the trip? Jeez, Larry, you haven't been out in weeks."

"I've been swimming every day since you left, and I'm on a new therapy."

"What kind of therapy?"

Larry wriggled a little against the pillow, and Earl rose up, his back arched. "You ever meet Marla, the massage therapist down in the basement at the centre? She does this thing with energy channels."

Mel groaned. "You had major surgery to open your channels. Don't tell me you're paying someone for mumbo jumbo."

"What have I got to lose? And for your information, Marla says I'm a perfect candidate for this therapy."

"Of course she told you that. To a hammer everything looks like a nail." He tilted his head and squinted at Larry. "Marla with the energy isn't by any chance planning a holiday to Vegas, is she?"

Larry glared at him. "Shame on you. That sounds like something Louise would say." He stroked Earl's lumpy back. "I just want one last trip, is all."

"Jeez, Larry! Don't go morbid on me. Fran, and then Marge with her stroke, and your brother two years ago, and my brother before that. We gotta slow things down here."

A funny sad little smile played across Larry's five o'clock shadow. "Can't turn time around, pal. I know where I stand, and the ground's been shaky for a long time. But hey." He slapped his hands on the arms of the chair and Earl leapt up in protest, then circled twice and settled again. "Much as Fran's friends, your dearly beloved included, are pissed off with the arrangement, I'm not the one who died. And even though I'd have traded places with Fran in the blink of an eye if I could, I can't. So I'm gonna make the most of what I've got. And I'm pretty sure Fran would approve. Will you look in on Earl?"

Mel chewed on his lip, nodded, shrugged. "Sure." He glanced at his watch. "I'd better get moving."

Larry stood up with Earl in his arms. The cat squirmed, and walked his way up Larry's chest until he was sprawled over his shoulder.

At the door, when Mel bent to tie his shoes, his knees

creaked in protest. He straightened slowly and zipped up his jacket. "So when are you off to Vegas?"

Larry ran his hand through his hair. Looked like he'd just had a haircut. A little longer on the sides than usual —a hint of the sideburns he'd sported back in the sixties—definitely trimmed and styled.

"Soon as I can get a good seat sale," Larry said. "Want to meet me at the gym in the morning? Sounds like the knee could use oiling."

"I'll pick you up at ten . . . " But then Mel stopped. "You don't need me to ferry you around, do you?"

Larry shook his head. "I'll be fine."

Mel clapped a hand on his buddy's shoulder, gave a quick squeeze, and stepped into the cold.

On the way home, he imagined Louise meeting him at the door. She'd ask how Larry was doing. And he'd tell her it was hard. Damned hard. Then he'd tell her about Earl, and how Larry needed to get away and how he'd be going over there every day to feed the cat. But he wouldn't tell her about Earl chowing down on her chili, or about Larry's energy channels. And he'd wait until Larry was back to tell her he wasn't delivering any more hot meals.

Mel pulled into the driveway, parked, and stepped down from the truck. Damn knees. Maybe a little massage therapy would be just the ticket. Marla, eh? When he looked up, Louise was standing in the open door.

PRIMA PELICAN

I want to take Jean to the river, now, straight from the airport, and show her pelicans. There's just enough time before dark. She shakes her head, "I need food," she says, "and sleep. In that order. Why are you dressed like that?" She squints as though she's just noticed that I'm wearing a skirt, silk shirt, linen jacket. All borrowed from my daughter, except for the pantyhose and open-toed dress shoes. The same clothes that got her through job interviews a few months ago. The only difference is that Alana is now employed and I'm not.

"This is my job search costume. I didn't have time to go home and change. And please don't tell me what you think. Or that I look like Alana."

She leans back and closes her eyes. "I think I need to take you shopping. And that it's a good thing I didn't stay away any longer."

"Forget about me and my bad clothes," I say, "and tell me about your mom, and how terrible it was."

Jean has come back from England where she spent two months watching her mother die, disposing of the ashes of that life while I dealt with the wreckage of mine. She flew away a month after Glenn walked out on me, and because she's the only friend in whom I ever confide, I filled the gap with long walks by the river and cheap rosé. I could afford a slightly better vintage than what I've been buying, but I've gone nostalgic and reverted to the Mateus we guzzled in our student days. Glenn decided that his half of the household goods included our last few bottles of fine wine from the racks in the basement.

"Why would you even care?" he asked when he was dragging his belongings out the door. "You never appreciated the good stuff."

"I do now," I said.

When the rented van pulled away that day, hauling Glenn's share of our twenty-five years of life to the townhouse he was inhabiting with Jocelyn, I convinced myself that what I felt was relief. I wouldn't have to listen to the Rankin Family, read the *National Post*, or sniff his Eddie Bauer shirts for her perfume ever again. Relief. But then I opened the door of the double garage and stared at the concrete rectangle of floor where Glenn's car should have been and recognized the dull ache as something else entirely. I had never lived alone. From my parents' house to married students' quarters. From a couple to a family six months later. And until the sudden affluence of our middle-age, never a spare room or even a spare inch unoccupied. If I'd ever wished for space, it wasn't for thirty-six square feet of garage floor, or a bedroom all my own.

Over time, I moved my own car farther and farther from the wall until I was parking in the centre of the garage. And I began to migrate to the centre of the bed. Just when I felt as though every last molecule of Glenn had been annihilated from the house, he called and left a message asking for a meeting.

I erased his voice, turned off the answering machine, crumpled the notes he left tacked to the front door, the bathroom mirror, and my pillow, changed the locks, and trudged miles of riverbank. I lost Glenn and found pelicans. Most days I'm able to see that as a good trade.

The morning of that first sighting I'd driven down to the off-leash park by the river, stiff from a sleepless night. By the time I crossed the open field I could feel a revival in my muscles. Then I spotted the eagle in the top of a dead poplar on the other side of the river, and it wasn't until I stepped off the bridge and took the first steps along the bank that I paid attention to the flock of white on the water. A dozen pelicans bobbed with the gulls like prehistoric relatives come to visit. They sat high on the deep green water of July, necks neatly curled, long beaks aligned with the shore. I blinked and squinted while they floated in a water ballet, one bird larger than the rest leading the dance. I fished my binoculars from my pocket. Before I could focus, I was almost bowled over by a Golden Retriever bounding into the current. The prima pelican raised her wings, danced over the water with great yellow feet and, in three strokes of her wings, lifted at an easy angle to the river with the rest of her company following in a whoosh of white.

I walked back to the car, so lost in the memory of black-edged wings against cloudless blue, that I didn't notice a man leaning on the front fender until I took my first crunching step onto the gravel in the parking lot. Glenn.

"What are you doing here?" I folded my arms and clenched them tight to my waist. We reached the driver's door at the same time. Glenn looked as though he intended to bar my way. I wedged myself between him and the car, dragged the keys from the pocket of my jeans with one hand, and swung the other elbow at his chest.

He leapt away before I could connect. I opened the car, slid behind the wheel and slammed the door.

"Answer your phone messages and I won't have to come looking for you," he shouted. I almost expected him to pound on the window, even though that sort of physical aggression would have been totally out of character. Instead, he planted his fists on his hips.

He looked exactly like our son when he was about ten years old, wanting desperately to scream but knowing his cause was doomed if he gave in to the temptation. Finally, I rolled down the window. "What do you want, Glenn?"

The morning sun behind him was blindingly bright, his face a shadow with a glimmering halo of hair. He bent down, long fingers gripping the edge of the window, the tendons in his hand pulled tight into a fan of cords. "We need to talk about wrapping things up. You have to find a lawyer, Beth. If you don't want to go back to the house we can go for coffee."

Sit across from him. Sip coffee and talk about divorce. About selling the house. Not a chance. I was not ready to be reasonable. I wanted to stay angry.

I whipped my head around, stared out the windshield, clenched my jaw and drew desperately on images of Jocelyn. I would have expected Glenn to choose a swan, someone beautiful and serene, not this gaudy peacock. I'd only seen her twice, but she was burned onto my brain like the scorch mark on the last of Glenn's shirts I ever ironed. On the odd occasions that I wore lipstick, it was a pale shade called Barely There, not even remotely in the same colour range as the red stain on the shoulder of that white shirt. I'd held the iron over the spot until the shirt began to smoke.

"No," I said. "Back off!" This time he took me seriously and stepped away before the car shot backwards in a spray of gravel.

At dusk, I went to the river again. There were twenty-two pelicans. I wrote to Jean that night with such a gushing account of wings and beaks that she phoned the day she got the letter to ask if I'd lost my mind. I promised to show her the pelicans as soon as she was back.

Jean's kept her eyes closed for the last five minutes, head back, but she's not asleep. "Food," she repeats.

"They don't feed you even on overseas flights?"

"Please!" She shudders. "We won't call that food." Now she sits up and turns to stare into my face. "About your kinship with these birds you've been babbling about in your letters. Beth, you are not a pelican. You look like Audrey Hepburn. Even now, with that terrible haircut. Glenn always said he married you because you looked like Audrey Hepburn. Pelicans are pouchy, big-beaked, goofy looking monstrosities with bad hair."

"Maybe I'm tired of having a perky hairdo. And the snazzy little black dresses in my closet are even less appropriate for job interviews than the jeans and sweaters Glenn says make me look like a recycled teenager. Pelicans have grace and dignity," I say. "I'll show you. Tomorrow or whenever you finally wake up. Where do you want to eat?"

"Just take me home. We'll order pizza from the place downstairs."

I've been hoping to get through the evening without mentioning Glenn, but already he's riding along with us in the car. Now Jean taps the ring on my left hand. "Why are you still wearing that?"

Because if I tugged it off, what would I do with it then?

"Because one of these days I'll be desperate enough to stop at Cash Converters and I'll need to have it with me." I can tell from the expression on Jean's face that she's not buying. She knows that I can't let go. Not quite.

"What happened to the job at that private school?"

"Not even an interview for that one. The public board says they'll keep me on the substitute list, but there's nothing full-time. I can blow my hair dry at six o'clock every morning and sit and wait for the phone to ring. Maybe." I don't want to tell her about today's interview. And how excited I was when the smiling woman said they'd love to have me join their team. But unfortunately the staff training job I'd applied for had already been filled. Would I be interested in a position in marketing? Telemarketing. No, I won't tell Jean that on the drive to the airport I wondered if I'd made a mistake in turning it down.

I execute a sloppy parallel park in front of Jean's building. Drop my hands from the wheel and turn to look at her. "Did you know," I ask, "that pelicans don't mate for life like Canada geese? They only stay together until the kids leave the nest. Then they're free. Whether they want it that way or not."

"They're rapidly gaining my respect," she says.

We carry her luggage inside. I'm surprised there isn't more. I expected her to come back with a load of her mother's belongings. Jean takes a padded hanger from the front hall closet and carefully hangs her jacket. She lifts her hair with an upward swoop of her fingers, stretches, then sniffs the sleeve of her silk shirt. "I need to wash my face, and change clothes. I smell like the man who was sitting next to me on the plane. The pizza menu's beside the phone and there's a bottle of Valpolicello somewhere in the kitchen."

I've ordered the pizza, opened the wine and carried it into the living room by the time she comes back in jeans and clean sweater looking as though she's scrubbed her cheeks with a facecloth. I kick off my shoes and sit facing the wide expanse of window. The white leather sofa ripples and sighs under my weight. Far below us, the reflection of downtown Calgary dances in the black mirror of the Bow River.

"This is such a pretty place," I muse. "I wonder if I could be happy in an apartment." An idle question. The only apartment I could afford would be a little bachelor nest on the main floor, facing south into a concrete wall. And I have pelican tendencies. I was pleased when I looked them up in my bird book and found the description of the trampled, poorly defined edges of the nest. The difference is that both sexes build the nest together. Glenn spent twenty-five years squinting tight-lipped at my shoddy housekeeping, but retreating to his own pristine den rather than lifting a hand to help or even telling me how much he hated the mess. I thought it was a healthy sign that we never fought. Oddly, both our kids keep tidy houses and seem to know how to communicate with their partners.

Jean sips her wine and regards me thoughtfully over the rim of the glass. "Would you be happy in this apartment?"

I have to grip the edges of the skin-soft cushions, because the dark world outside Jean's window suddenly tilts. It's been more than twenty years since we taught at the same school. I invited Jean to have dinner with us about a week after she arrived. Even though we lived in a small rented house, had two kids, and were still paying off Glenn's students loans, we entertained often in those days. Just spaghetti, I warned her, and she showed up with a bottle of good red wine. We had to dig the cork out with a knife, because we didn't own a cork screw. Our wine came in big bottles with screw caps. Jean had a classy accent, was beautiful, wickedly funny, and a perfect match, I thought, for my brother. So I invited him too. He drove Jean home and never mentioned her again, but the next day at school, Jean laid a manicured hand on my sleeve and whispered that she'd be more interested if I had a sister. I looked around to see who was within earshot. This was the seventies.

"Oh don't look so worried," she said, when I struggled to swallow. "You're not my type. But I do want to be your friend."

Now she's asking if I could imagine living here, in her apartment, and I feel as though I'm back in that old staff room, tiptoeing on ice. "Why are you asking me this?"

"Because I've decided to go back to London as soon as I get some things settled here. For a couple of months anyway. And then I'll decide if I'm going to make it permanent. Meanwhile, I have a lease. Sell your house, Beth, and I'll sublet to you at a rent you can afford."

I'm about to ask if there's someone in London when the pizza man rings the bell. While Jean lets him up and waits at the door I get plates and napkins.

Jean wolfs down two slices of pizza, but manages, as always, to look as though she's dining at the palace. I rearrange the olives and red onion on my own piece and pick at a lump of feta cheese. "I'm not sure I want to sell the house."

"Oh for God's sake, Beth. A house is just a house."

I ignore her. She's told me this before. At least twice in the long phone calls we've had these three months she's been away. I tilt my head back and look only at the sky. "It would be so much easier if Glenn had died. People would have brought casseroles and sympathy instead of wondering what I did to drive him away. The house would be all mine, and I'd have his lovely insurance money to pay the bills."

Jean sniffs. "Yes, and you'd stay in the house wallowing in memories forever."

"I'm not wallowing," I snap. And I sit up. "I'm talking about my home. Just because Glenn can't stand living with me anymore he gets to turn the whole damn thing upside down. Not only his half, but mine too. I always thought I'd live there forever."

She frowns. "Beth, that is so depressing. Be thankful he's gone. The sooner you move on, the better."

The sky is churning foamy grey clouds against the black. Rain pelts the glass. I stand, peer through my distorted reflection to the circus of lights below and step back. "Maybe I'll forget about apartments. Heights have always made me dizzy."

She sips and shrugs. "You'll get used to it."

"I'm used to where I live." I expect her to tell me again that this is my problem. This pathetic clinging to what I used to have. But she's oddly silent, watching me with her head tilted, a finger to her lips. The chill is gone from the room now, and I'd like to take off my jacket and sink back onto the couch. As a matter of fact, in this warm apartment with lamps on in every corner, Jean finally here again, I realize that I don't want to leave. But it's late and she's been up since yesterday. "Now that you're fed, I'll go and you can sleep."

She walks me to the door. When she hugs me, I smell the fatigue of the journey on her skin. She steps away and folds her arms. "There's another possibility you know." When I wait for her to continue, she looks down at her bare feet, at shell pink toes, for maybe twenty seconds and then she finds me again with the familiar calculating smile. Only the rapid blinking gives her away. "You could come with me. To London."

I nod. "I could. But that would change everything.

And I can't bear any more change." I touch my cheek to hers one more time.

"I know," she says. "Forget that I asked. We'll hunt pelicans tomorrow."

The storm has passed. Out on the sidewalk, I crane my neck for a glimpse of sky but the towering buildings block the stars. I press against the wall to let people by, my ears ringing with the babble of their talk, their confident, teasing, going-somewhere talk. They pass so close I can smell the heavy reek of food and booze, of cigarettes and bodies hot for the night ahead. So close their tripping feet splash rain across my toes.

I dodge the shiny puddles and wait for a break in traffic before I unlock the car door and slip behind the wheel. My foot is heavy. The car eats up the blocks of splashing pavement and barely pauses for breath at the ON ramp to Deerfoot Trail. As the freeway winds south through the broad valley, the moon appears, hung high over the river, a thread of cloud wisped across the gold.

The closer I get to home, the slower I drive, aware that everyone on the road is passing me. And it's not that I want to be back with Jean, I realize with a jolt, but that I don't want to go home. Not yet. Instead of turning uphill to the lights, the streets, the safety of the garage, I'm drawn to the moonlight and the swirls of fog in the valley. I steer to the park by the river, pull into the empty parking lot and sit.

There was another time Glenn followed me to the river. A morning in April when I was still trying to ignore the clues—so many more besides the residue of lipstick and perfume. Jean had told me bluntly a week earlier, after I confided my fears, to stop being pathetic. That Glenn wasn't stupid, and was deliberately laying a trail, hoping I'd grab hold of some dignity and toss him out. I'd stared back at her, thinking that she couldn't possibly understand. She hadn't any idea what was at stake. Or that there'd been other times in the twenty-five years when I'd had niggling doubts rather than real clues, and stuck my head under my wing and sat tight on the nest waiting for him to come back. He always did. He could iron his own shirts from now on, but I was still sure he'd be back. We'd glide graciously into old age as the couple I'd always imagined us. At a New Year's Eve party, I'd catch his eye from across the room, wink, and people around us would envy our private joke. Later, when it was time to toast the new year, he'd wait until everyone else had their champagne to their lips and then raise his glass to me with a special smile. The stuff of old movies. Audrey Hepburn and Cary Grant.

I'd gone to bed before Glenn that night, still arguing with Jean in my mind. His den was across the hall from the bedroom. Normally, I'd hear the glide of the desk drawer, the shuffle of paper, the click of the lamp beside his reading chair. That night there was leaden silence. No whisper of pages, no creaking shift of the chair, no clearing of his throat or rearranging of his long legs. I dozed, and suddenly he was there in bed, but absolutely still beside me in the dark. I turned to face him and rested my fingers against his cheek.

"Glenn?" I whispered.

I felt him nod just once against my hand. When he was still silent, I slid close, and buried my face in

194

his shoulder. The feel of his skin against mine and the smell of him steadied my heart to a quiet thud. Familiar ripples spread through me like footsteps on a path I could have travelled with my eyes closed. I shifted a warm leg to rest between his, waiting for his hands on my skin. The same journey for twenty-five years; a landscape I wanted to believe was as secure and necessary to me as my river walks.

He eased away, leaving me sprawled on the sheet that was barely warm from his body. And though it wasn't a first, his turning away, I was left this time with Jean's voice, hard and flat in my mind. Pathetic. I took some bedding to the living room and curled on the sofa with my knees tight to my chest and a fistful of blanket against my mouth.

In the morning Glenn brought me coffee as though that room was my usual waking place. The sun shone, the nubbly grey sweater he wore was one I'd given him for Christmas, the room rumpled around us like a comfortable old sock and I let myself believe I'd had a nightmare.

"If you're walking this morning, Beth, I'll come with you. I'm taking the day off."

I was astounded. If we ever we came close to fighting, it was because Glenn never took time off. Even on a Sunday morning he would go back to the office, or hole up in his den. Most of the mutual friends who'd crowded into our small long-ago kitchen for chili dinners had long since moved on. We never entertained at home anymore, although there were plenty of obligatory restaurant dinners with Glenn's clients. In a rare confrontation, I'd once questioned whether the marketing of sulphur was an essential service. Surely there was time for a day in Banff, or brunch with friends. Old friends. People who laughed at my bad jokes. He'd turned and walked out of the room. And I'd driven over to Jean's and paced up and down in front of the expanse of sky behind her window, alternating my ranting with weeping.

Before our walk, I showered and dressed and Glenn read the paper in the garden. I watched him from the kitchen window while I drank another cup of coffee. There were robins all atwitter, flying back and forth to a nest in the willow tree over his head.

Later, when I went out to the car, he was waiting in the passenger seat. The radio was on, Peter Gzowski's compassionate Morningside voice painting the grim picture of the Red River rampaging through southern Manitoba. River rising, wiping out everything in its muddy path. We'd watched the frantic sandbagging the night before on The Journal. Glenn had wondered if his brother in Winnipeg was affected, and I'd worried about nests swept away on the flood.

We locked the car in the parking lot, and shuffled along in silence until we crossed the river and clambered down a sandy bank.

I turned my back on the muddy water. It slid along, a mellow milk chocolate, deceptively still except when a madly bobbing chunk of tree tore past.

"What is it you're itching to tell me, Glenn? You didn't come along to keep me company."

He looked away, over my shoulder, with such deliberate interest that I whirled. The river was the same rippling sheet, like an ugly brown stain spreading across the day.

"I'm leaving, Beth. There's no easy way to say this. There's someone else, but even if there wasn't it would still be time to call it quits."

Now his eyes slid back to mine and I stared at him, mute. He held out a hand when I began to back away. "Beth, please. We have to talk about this. For once, we have to talk."

The outstretched hand was more than I could bear. I took a step toward him, raised my arm and swung a clenched fist into his palm. And then I ran. Up the bank, along the path. I ran until I was hidden in the trees where I dropped, the new grass tickling my cheek and the primal smell of boiling river so strong I dug my nails into the wet earth and wished I had the courage to howl.

The smell of the water reaches me now even through glass. I let the car idle, roll down the window. Never have I seen this place by moonlight.

I open the door, step into the damp night and button my linen jacket. The bark chip path shines silver, stretching a crooked trail across the field to the river, and my heels sink through the wood into soft earth. I kick out of these ridiculous shoes and slip one into each pocket of my coat, peel off my pantyhose and lob the silky ball into the wet grass.

The slivers of bark cut like shards of ice. By the time I step onto the pedestrian bridge, my feet are numb. The concrete barely registers the soft sound of my footfall.

At the centre of the bridge, I lean over the railing, playing my fingertips across the outside of the cold metal bars. A gust of wind lifts the hem of my skirt, and from the rippling surface below, swirls of mist rise to my face. I rub my hands to warm them but catch, with each overlay and linking of fingers, the edges of my wedding ring.

I tug the gold band across my knuckle and into my palm. Stare down at diamonds circled together to form the heart of a rose. Turning, I slide my back down the metal bars to sit and draw my knees up, skirt folded and tucked around my legs, bare feet flat on wet cement. I slip the ring from hand to hand, one fingertip, then another. Without the ring the fingers of my right hand might play endlessly, nervously with the band of flesh that feels dead and white.

From the far side of the river, a flash of light illuminates the bank. A burst of laughter, a shout and then an eruption of Tarzan whoops from a party of teenagers as the pile of wood catches fire. My first date with Glenn was a party at his fraternity house and later a bonfire in Emily Murphy Park. Apparently, well into the night, I'd climbed a tree and sung the university anthem to the sky, ending with a mini strip-tease. Glenn told me his frat brothers had voted me "sexiest girl at the party." After Glenn's last staff Christmas party, he told me I sounded unbalanced when I tried to convince people to go carolling down the street.

I used to know parties like the one on the river bank. When the last beer can is flung, there, under the trees where Glenn whined out the sad ending to our marriage, they'll piss out the fire.

I push up from the bridge with the palm of one hand. In the other, the ring presses a cold circle against my skin. The laughter from the party is now a murmur barely audible over the crackling fire and the gurgle and slosh of river against the bridge pilings. The revellers have sorted themselves into pairs and stand around the fire leaning into one other, inky two-headed silhouettes.

I straighten, grip the chipped railing and stare downstream at an island, scrubby brush rising in lacy frills, long grass rippling black within the dark circle. I conjure a lone pelican, huddled against the shore, neck curled, head tucked safely beneath her wing. Not likely, I think, because pelicans are highly gregarious. But this is a pelican of my own imagining and I'm giving her a quiet night on the river. There's no reason for her to go home to that scruffy nest. Chicks are gone, her mate is history.

In a month or two, Jean will be back in London. On the walk back to the car, instead of steeling myself for my own dark living room, I envision Jean's living room, white leather sofa warmed with my mother's crocheted afghan, a pile of books and a tea pot on the glass coffee table, and the drapes drawn tight against the night. I could enjoy such a quiet night. But there will be others when the spaghetti sauce is simmering on Jean's state-of-the-art range top, and the room fills up with friends. Old friends I'm sure I can find if I dig out the Christmas card list. When I reach into my pocket for the keys to the car, I tuck my wedding ring into the deepest corner.

GETTING RID OF RUTH

For six months I had a recurring dream that my best friend had died. Then she did.

In my nightmares, I was always in Ruth's living room with her family. They were fighting over the furniture. I wanted desperately to leave the room but the only route out was through the kitchen, where Ruth's coffin blocked the way. Grant was never in the dreams, dead or alive. But then I didn't really know Grant. Not at all, as it turned out.

The seed of this bad dream was planted when Ruth called me last June. It was five-thirty, a time we've dubbed the witching hour at our house, and she could probably hear the pots and pans clanking and the kids fighting.

"I know this is a bad time," she said, "but I'm having premonitions."

"Ruth," I said, trying to slide a pan of potatoes into the hot oven with one hand, "you've had premonitions as long as I've known you. None of them ever bear fruit."

"I know, but this is the one they've been leading to, Theresa. This is the bad harvest." I would have laughed at the melodrama if the hair on the back of my neck hadn't quivered. "Move to a quieter place so you can pay attention," she said.

I grabbed a beer out of the fridge and a glass from the drain board. When I passed through the living room on my way to the front step, Andy looked up from the newspaper. I mouthed Ruth's name and he rolled his eyes.

Andy never liked Ruth. Shortly after we met, Ruth hired him to build cabinets in a bathroom she was renovating. He told me he'd never work for her again. She'd talked incessantly about encouraging me to go back to school, to finish the teaching degree I'd abandoned when we got married. It was as though, Andy said, he was standing in my way.

"Okay, it's quiet," I said, settling onto the concrete step with the cordless phone tucked under my chin. "What?" I poured half the beer and left the rest in the bottle for Andy.

"Grant and I are writing a new will before we go to Vancouver this weekend, in case we drive off a mountain. We want you to be our executor." I set the glass down. I'm sure she heard me swallow. "Don't talk yet," she said. Not much chance. I was speechless. "It won't be all that hard. There's lots of money and Steven's old enough to look after himself so long as someone watches over him for the first few years."

"Ruth. That doesn't make sense. You and Grant have family."

"No. They can't be trusted. I've discussed this with Grant. You're the only one."

There was no talking her out of it. So I agreed.

Andy was aghast. "Do you have any idea what sort of a mess that woman could leave behind? You already know about the illegitimate kid, and that her sisters are nut cases and her in-laws won't have anything to do with her. And last but not least, you seem to be her only friend, and sweetheart, there's a reason for that."

I so regretted telling Andy that Ruth had given up a baby. He'd been complaining about the amount of time I spent with her, and I'd tried to explain why I appreciated her company, how we had so much in common.

I first met Ruth in a beginners' swimming class. I was terrified of deep water, but determined to keep up with my three pre-schoolers. My five-year-old was already puppy-swimming in water twice his depth. Andy had suggested the swimming lessons. It would be good for me to get out, he said. We'd just moved to Calgary from Winnipeg, and he was afraid I'd become a social isolate. For four years I'd given all my energy to a search for my birthmother, and lost all interest in friends.

Ruth said she'd grown up in a backwoods town with no money for lessons even if there'd been a swimming pool. After bluffing for years, she wanted to cut a graceful figure in the pool on an upcoming Christmas cruise. The young instructor had three months to whip her into shape, she said.

The other four women in the group were way ahead

of us. They kicked their flutter boards into the deep end, while Ruth and I lay on our backs in two feet of water. And sank repeatedly. Heavy bones, the bemused instructor told us after trying everything in his watery bag of tricks to keep us afloat. And how strange to have two people in the same class share a problem he rarely encountered.

We giggled in the change room later. Then we went for coffee and sat for two hours talking as easily as sisters. Andy was frantic by the time I got home, but pleased when I told him I'd made a friend. Ruth had invited me to lunch.

It was naïve of me to assume that Ruth lived in a cookie cutter house like mine. Her clothes, her jewellery, the cruise she was planning should have been clues. But her stories about growing up in a logging town in northern Alberta ran parallel to my own hometown tales. I felt like we'd been neighbours, two provinces apart, even though Ruth was ten years older.

I sat outside in my car on that September afternoon, checking the address, staring at the elegant sandstone house, feeling too intimidated to ring the bell. On a Sunday not long before, Andy and I had driven through this neighbourhood, where back yards sloped to the Elbow River, and joked about lottery tickets.

A young boy was flying a remote control helicopter on the sweep of front lawn. He came running to the car to say that he was Steven and, if I was Theresa, I should go around back. His mom was in the garden.

Seated at a wrought iron bistro table on a patio blazing with pots of bronze chrysanthemums, Ruth and I picked up where we'd left off at Tim Horton's. After my second glass of wine I told her I'd begun searching for my birthmother the year my adoptive mother died. How the search had ended. She sat perfectly still on the filigree chair, let her eyes flick to the house, and then leaned forward.

"Listen to me, Theresa," she said. "The woman probably has good reasons, and you should respect her decision." It would be another two years before she told me she'd given up a baby girl when she was seventeen.

At the end of that first of many visits to the sandstone house, Ruth showed me the canvasses in her studio. She painted her back yard over and over, season by season and I was never sure if the garden or the images were the greater works of art.

A week after the morbid phone call, when she was safely home from Vancouver, Ruth invited me once again to lunch in her garden.

Although it was late September, there hadn't been a killing frost and the wide path to the river was bordered by arching stems of daylily and a blue haze of flax. Since my first visit to Ruth's garden, I'd nagged Andy to give up a square of our manicured lawn to a flower bed, but he was immoveable, as attached to his grass as he was to his dislike of Ruth. As well as complaining that I spent more time with Ruth than I did at home, which was blatantly untrue, he said that Ruth had become the most influential person in my life, which was probably correct.

We had barely touched our shrimp salads when Ruth started in on the will.

"Grant's brothers are always working on a new

scheme," she said, "and they'll try to convince Steven to invest with them. If they get even a toe in the door he'll lose all this for sure." Her eyes flickered from the house to the garden to the gentle river. "My sister, Louise, is weird as the wind. She lives like a gypsy. I'm afraid she'll move in with Steven. She'll fill the house with dubious people—she gathers lost souls—and he'll be too polite to kick them out." She shuddered visibly. "I can imagine what this place would look like after a month of Louise's habitation. If she tries to settle in, you tell her to get lost, Theresa. You have to be very firm with Louise, even if you like her. She has this charismatic way, and sucks people in."

I could imagine Andy's response to that one. "Don't worry," I told Ruth. "I can be tough."

I wondered how Steven had reacted to all of these plans. Or if Ruth had even told him. In the years I'd known Steven, he'd grown from a boy to a knobby adolescent, and then into a confident, funny young man, a university student with a gift for math and a passion for climbing mountains and canoeing white water. I imagined him blowing off his mother's soothsaying with a breezy wave of the hand.

"Your job is to keep the family at bay. Steven should stay in the house. It's a good investment." Ruth held up the bottle of wine, but I shook my head. She refilled her glass. "We've done a list of small bequests but everything else belongs to Steven."

I glanced around the garden, toward the house where sunlight bounced off a solid wall of glass. All this for one boy. My own three would be lucky if our mortgage was paid out by the time they inherited.

Then Ruth started on the funeral. "My mother-in-law will want to plan the party. Where Grant's concerned," she'd said, "let the old bat have her way. But nix anything my sisters plan. I don't want to lie in a box with glum faces hanging over me. Esther's been a pain in the ass since she was saved. Tell her if all the praying she's done for me so far hasn't helped it'll be way too late when I'm dead. Cremation. Get rid of me and keep it cheap."

"Look," I said, "you're giving me the creeps. Can we stop talking about this? You're safely home. So much for premonitions."

Ruth fiddled with the silverware in front of her. "No, that one didn't come true. Not yet." She put her salad fork aside and smoothed the linen placemat. "But there's this other problem. My daughter has found me. Or rather I've been found by an adoption agency looking on her behalf."

There was no way I could have prepared myself for the anger that almost shot me out of my chair as she spoke. From the beginning of the story, it was clear she had no intention of meeting this child.

Finally, she folded her arms and sat back. "They say she grew up in a good family, she's doing fine, and she just wants information. I told them to send me a questionnaire."

"Ruth!" I gripped the edge of the table, rocking it on the stone patio. "I had a family that was as healthy as anyone can hope for, but as long as I can remember I've fantasized about the woman who gave me up. Over and over I imagined a door opened by someone who looked just like me. You know how devastated I was

206

when I found that door locked and barred." My voice cracked. But she seemed to be listening, so I paused for breath, then raged on. "How can you brush your own child away with a questionnaire? You don't have to let them release anything that identifies you," I said. I was an expert on the subject. "But meet with her and answer her questions. At least give her that."

"I'll think about it," she said.

Two days later, she phoned. "That agency called back," she said. "Okay, this is a one-shot deal and you're coming with me. Theresa, you are sworn to secrecy. Absolute secrecy."

Ruth's daughter, Karen, flew to Calgary from Ottawa for the reunion. Ruth arranged to meet her at a restaurant she'd never been to before and would never visit again. She told Karen she'd be wearing a fedora and sitting with a nervous-looking blonde.

Karen spotted us instantly and wove her way through the tables looking like a young Ruth, black hair brushing the shoulders of her crimson silk shirt. A woven bag hung from her arm. After stumbled introductions, she sat down and stared boldly at Ruth, from hat, to wild silver-streaked hair, to the black shawl splashed with poppies on her shoulders, jingling silver bracelets on her wrists, long fingers that couldn't stop rearranging the silverware and tracing patterns in the condensation on her water glass.

Finally Karen opened her bag, pulled out a notebook and flipped through the pages. She pushed it across the table to Ruth. "These are the things I don't know," she said, "and that might be important some day. You left a

207

lot of blanks when you filled out my adoption forms."
Then she sat back, folded her arms and waited.

Ruth glanced at the sheet of paper, then stared back
at Karen. "I was seventeen years old. I didn't know the
answers." She leaned on her elbows, chin in her hands,
and bent over the page. After a minute of alternately
nodding, then slowly shaking her head she looked up.
"Diabetes, yes, on both sides of my family. Heart problems, yes, but just the men. No to everything else except
mental illness. My whole family is crazy. But I'm fine,
so you're probably safe." She closed the book. "If you
promise you won't take notes," she said, "I'll tell you
about the summer I hitchhiked to Quebec and worked
at a lodge in the Laurentians. I met this dreamboat
named Alain. I never did learn to spell his last name
or even pronounce it. I never saw or heard from him
again. You won't find him, so don't waste your time."

Ruth answered questions, but asked none. When
she was done with picking through her salad, she got
up to go to the Ladies' room. "Theresa's adopted too,"
she said. "The two of you can compare notes while I'm
gone."

Had it been me, I couldn't have walked across that
room. I'd have caved in as soon as I stood. But Ruth
floated loose-limbed the way she always did.

Karen exhaled. "I didn't think it would be so hard,"
she said. "Was it this hard for you?"

"My mother signed a veto." I didn't tell Karen how
lucky she was. That I knew from a social worker's carefully chosen words that my mother was not the fairy
princess I'd dreamed. The kind woman who tracked
her down urged me to drop the search and under no

208

circumstances to begin one for my birthfather. If I'd told Karen all of that, she might have seen through my pathetic need to transfer my fairy tale to her reunion with Ruth.

I pushed away my half-eaten sandwich. While we waited, I asked the questions Ruth should have asked. Karen was an only child of doting parents who'd helped her finance the search for Ruth. She'd graduated from the Ontario College of Art and Design, worked in a gallery. I bit my tongue so hard to keep from telling her about Ruth's work that I tasted blood.

When Ruth came back, I mentioned ever so quietly while I stirred my coffee that Karen was an artist. Ruth carefully set her cup on its saucer. "That's interesting. I wonder if Alain has a creative streak." She pushed away from the table. "I'm awfully sorry, Karen, but I have to go now."

Karen scrabbled in her bag for a piece of paper. "Here. This is my address, and my phone number, and my number at work." She looked as though she'd fly off the chair and land in Ruth's lap if she made another move. "And the address at the bottom is my parents'," she said. "I'm going out to the east coast for the summer, but they could put you in touch."

Ruth took the piece of paper, folded it. "You really shouldn't count on me," she said. She stood, hesitated, opened her arms to Karen for the briefest of embraces, and then we left. In the car, she handed me the phone number.

"Throw it away," she said.

"But you didn't even tell her about Steven. Shouldn't she know she has a brother?"

"No! I don't want her nosing around in my life. Steven and I have a wonderful relationship. I will not compromise that." I'd never heard Ruth raise her voice. Nor had I seen her so visibly rattled. Her hand shook when she raised it to fix her hair. She glanced from the rear view mirror to the window as though she was afraid Karen might be running toward us. "I answered her questions. That was more for you than it was for her and it was definitely not for me."

"How can you bear to live in a lie?"

She stared me down. "Get over it, Theresa."

"Not likely," I told her quietly.

"Well, that's up you, I guess. But this secret belongs to you too. You remember that."

I would not be allowed to forget. I kept the address and phone number, sure Ruth would change her mind, that I'd change it for her, but three months later her grim prediction came true.

Ruth and Grant were caught in a white-out on their way home from Ruth's opening at a gallery in Edmonton—one of the freaky storms that seem to lurk in the valley around Red Deer—and piled into the back of a parked tow truck. Since the Vancouver trip, they'd flown to Toronto and to San Diego and she'd called both times with premonitions. Ruth, I thought much later, would have felt cheated if she'd known that it wasn't a mountain road or a fiery plane crash she'd foretold. Just a slippery drive home to Calgary on a boring stretch of road, and an unfortunate collision.

Grant's funeral was packed. At the front of the chapel, the spotlit urn of his ashes looked oddly like an Aladdin's lamp. It was the sort of thing Ruth would have chosen with a glint in her eye, but it was Grant's mother who'd made the final arrangements.

She'd honoured Ruth's wishes to the letter by ignoring her. There wasn't a trace of Ruth beyond the mention in the service folder that she, Grant's beloved wife, had perished with him.

Andy had surprised me the night before by offering to come along to the funeral. The sisters, Louise and Esther, who I'd met two days earlier in Ruth's living room in a scene eerily true to my nightmare, huddled together in the vestibule. I guessed there were other members of Ruth's family present, but my mind was on the one who was missing. I hadn't called Karen.

Through the short service, I leaned deeper and deeper into Andy's comforting bulk. I was even more grateful for his presence later when Ruth's sisters waylaid us as we tried to make a quick exit.

Louise was an older, wilder version of Ruth, eyes so rimmed with red it hurt to look at her. "Theresa, they told us you're in charge. You have to tell Steven to save Ruth. Don't let them throw her away." She clutched at my shoulder.

Then Esther grabbed my hands. She was sobbing so hard, I was surprised she was able to speak. "At least a memorial service," she wailed through great gulps of sorrow. "Oh dear Lord, I don't want my sister to burn in hell!"

Andy put an arm around each of them and moved them gently aside. I would do what Ruth wanted, he assured them, and wasn't that what they wanted as well? And no, he said, we really couldn't come back to

211

the house with the family. As hard as this was for them, I had lost my best friend and needed some time alone.

The next day, I phoned Karen.

"I don't believe you," she said. "Not after it took me two years to find her."

"You've been hoping she'd change her mind?"

"Of course I have," she said. "You should understand that." I flinched.

"There isn't going to be a funeral for Ruth," I told her. As though she'd be inclined to attend. I couldn't imagine Karen sneaking into a back pew with a dark veil over her face. This is what I would have done.

Grant's mother stayed with Steven for the first month. I agreed with the family, even though Steven balked at the idea, that it wasn't healthy for him to be alone. Ruth had left detailed notes instructing him to find room-mates and fill the house with young people. "Maybe later," he said, "but I doubt it." He shook his head. "I'm surprised she even suggested that."

I'd stopped by at his grandmother's request. She was surrounded by boxes, enthroned on the same swivel chair in which she'd been seated on all my other vis-its to the house. "Steven and I have finished sorting Grant's personal things, and Steven's put aside every-thing he wants to keep. These boxes are coming home with me. Ruth's sisters can deal with her belongings. After I've gone." She pushed herself stiff-armed from the chair and left the room.

"That was difficult for both of you," I said. "I should have helped."

Steven looked up from where he knelt on the floor.

He pulled a square white box out of a larger carton. "What should I do with this?" I blinked at him, at the box, and my hand automatically reached out. "Grandma says she'll take Dad's urn."

Finally I understood, my arm whipping back across my chest to clutch my shoulder as though he'd flung the contents at me. "Steven!" I felt the lower half of my face twist. "Why was this left to you?" I knew Grant's mother had claimed his Aladdin's lamp, but I hadn't questioned the fate of Ruth's ashes. I'd assumed that the funeral home had done exactly as she asked and thrown her away. "I am so sorry," I whispered. I was furious with myself, with the family, and finally with Ruth. A twenty-year-old boy should not have to hold his mother's ashes in his hands. No child should have to do that.

"I'm sorry," I said again, shaking my head. "I haven't done my job. All your mom's careful plans and I haven't kept my promise."

For the first time the calm mask cracked. The cords in Steven's neck bulged and his face blotched with red. "She didn't have to make those goddamn plans or ask for promises. I don't want to hear anymore about her plans or her premonitions. My mother couldn't read tea leaves, and she didn't have a crystal ball. This was all just a fuckin' awful coincidence." He was gripping the box so tightly his knuckles shone in the dim room.

I grabbed it from his hands, surprised by the weight. "I'll take this with me," I said. "Don't even think about it for now. We'll come up with something." Then for the first time since I'd known this boy, I put my arms around him and held him as tightly as if he were one of my own.

Before I got into my car, I stashed the box in the trunk under the flap of carpet that covered the spare tire. I could imagine Andy's face if I walked into the house with Ruth's ashes.

The February chinook wind had uncovered signs of Ruth's fall planting. Small mounds and markers where tulips would bloom.

My job as executor was not nearly as onerous as Andy had predicted or as Ruth had led me to fear. Grant's lawyer had everything in hand. Steven's grandmother made certain of that. By the end of a month, she was anxious to get home to Toronto. The rest of the family, she was sure, must be floundering without her counsel. Meanwhile, she phoned every one of Grant and Ruth's acquaintances and created a roster for inviting Steven to dinner. She made him promise that he would spend at least two weeks with her in the summer. By the time she drove away, I'd become quite fond of the old lady.

Then Louise arrived to take her turn, and phoned me a few days later.

"Theresa, we need Ruth's ashes. I've brought Steven an urn, a jar that was our mother's."

"I don't think that was what Ruth had in mind, Louise. Could I speak to Steven?"

He was calm, even a little jaunty. "Yeah, sure. Bring the ashes. This will work out just fine."

I went over the next day, carrying the white box in a plastic shopping bag. On my way from the car to the house, the ashes grew heavier with every step. Stefan opened the door, took the bag from my hand and left it there on the floor.

We sat down in the kitchen and Louise came in a moment later carrying a pink jar. She placed it reverently on the table between us. It had a lid with a cut glass knob and was exactly like one my mother had owned. Depression glass. In our house, the jar had been perpetually filled with the hard Christmas candy that no one ever eats. The contents of the white box would fill at least three of those bowls.

I looked from the candy dish to the familiar velvet skirt and silk tunic Louise was wearing. "Oh." I felt the back of my throat tighten. "You look so much . . ."

"Just like Mom," Steven said, "in Mom's clothes. We cleaned out the closet. Aunty Louise is taking some of the stuff, and I thought we could give the rest to Aunty Esther's missionaries."

"Or we could just leave the rest here." Louise looked around the room as though she was searching for something, but wasn't quite sure what it was. "And whenever I come back, I can go through it again and take what I need." She smiled, pleased, it seemed, with her clever suggestion, but then the sad confusion returned. Poor Louise.

Steven put a hand on her arm. "Sure. Why don't you give me your keys, and I'll take the clothes out to the car. So you don't forget them tomorrow."

He left the room and was back in seconds with a huge suitcase. On his way out the door, he scooped up the plastic shopping bag.

I stayed just long enough to drink a cup of tea. Louise kept wandering out of the room, and in one of her longer absences, I got up to leave. Steven followed me outside with the candy dish in his hands.

"Is she really going tomorrow?" I asked.

He grimaced. "Maybe. If I can be mean enough. Mom never gave her more than three days, but I like having her around in a weird sort of way. The longer she stays, though, the harder it'll be to get rid or her."

"Isn't she going to insist that you put the ashes into the jar?" The scene was so bizarre, I felt myself on the verge of hysterics.

Steven pushed both of us over the edge. Mouth twitching, eyes wide, he stepped close and lowered his voice to a whisper. "My mother," he began, then sputtered, "would not fit into a candy dish, no matter how carefully we poured." After my moment of stunned silence, the two of us laughed until we were gasping for breath.

Finally, with the kind of relief that otherwise comes only after long weeping, we walked to my car. "By the time I go back inside," Steven said, "she'll have forgotten she even mentioned the ashes. I don't think the dish was my grandma's. Aunty Louise probably picked it up in someone else's house. If she surprises me and asks about it, I'll tell her I gave it to you." He handed me the pink glass. "I don't think she ever cleans out the trunk of that old car. It'll be years before she realizes she's now the custodian of the ashes."

At the end of March, a courier arrived at my house with a package from Louise. If she hadn't cushioned the white box in layers of bubble wrap and Styrofoam beads and sent it in an old computer carton, I might have guessed. The parcel was addressed to Steven in care of me, so I hauled it to the house by the river the next day, ignoring the weather warning. A spring blizzard was on its way.

Steven groaned when he slit open the tape and began digging through the bubbles. *I had to sell my car,* the note said, *and the man who bought it found this in the trunk. I'm so touched by Steven's trust, but it doesn't seem right. Ruth needs to be with Steven.*

"If only," I said, "in her zealousness to make all of this idiot-proof, your mother had told us exactly what to do with her ashes."

He looked at me oddly. "Do you think she ever got that far? I'm pretty sure she got off on the planning and the drama, but never went as far as thinking about dead bodies."

I sat down in his grandmother's favourite chair. No, Ruth could never have imagined the mother coming back to haunt the child. If she fantasized at all, she would have seen herself as a warm but fading mist of memory. Even knowing that I was carrying my own mother around like a suitcase with a lost key, even looking into Karen's desperate face when she took the address from her trembling hand, Ruth had believed that what was over was over.

I ripped a cocoon of bubble wrap off the box, and stomped through the house to the back door. Outside, the snow had begun to fall in great clumping flakes that clung to my hair. I slipped along the path to Ruth's potting shed with Steven trailing behind. Inside, the air smelled like cold deep earth. The collection of straw hats on the wall was silvered with frost. I stood on tiptoes to slide the box onto a shelf of garden chemicals.

In the house, I'd thought fleetingly of sending the ashes to Karen and asking her to choose Ruth's final resting place. The more I saw of Steven, the harder it had become to keep Ruth's secret. But that day, standing midst her garden tools, her flowered gloves hanging from a peg, my promises hung over me like knives.

I made it home just before the streets became impassable.

Steven seemed so mature and capable, I was unsure of what my job was supposed to be now that all the legal business seemed in order. I invited him to have supper with us one night, realizing, after I made the call, that in all the time I'd known her, Ruth had never been to my house. After we'd eaten, Andy dug out an extra baseball glove, and invited Steven to come along to the community ball diamond with the boys. I shouldn't have been surprised. Andy is a kind man, generous, easy-going. The only serious conflicts in our life had been around my feverish need to find my birth family, and his dislike of Ruth.

We stopped at the Dairy Queen on the way home. Our three boys had been hanging on Steven's every word, and the youngest, I noticed, even waited to see what flavour of sundae Steven ordered before he chose his own.

"Come again," Andy said at the end of the evening. "Any time. We have a spare bedroom if you ever need it."

"Thanks. It was fun." He looked a little shy with all of us clumped around him. "And for the offer of the bed, but I think I'm fine. When you're an only child

218

you get used to being alone. Most of the time I pretend that Mom and Dad are off on another holiday." I had to turn away and let the boys finish the good-bye.

The dream about the family vultures picking through Ruth's treasures seemed to have been banished by the reality. Now, I'd reverted to nightmares about finding my mother. Over and over again I knocked on a heavy door to find Ruth on the other side. When I reached out, her face melted away and I was left staring at my own image, but shrivelled and malevolent—a hag. Andy had claw marks on his arms. I woke up clinging to him.

Just before Steven's twenty-first birthday in November, he asked me to help him clean out the studio. The gallery had taken all of Ruth's paintings except for a few of Steven's favourites. He wanted me to choose one, and my heart had already leapt to a water colour of wildflowers. Steven stepped away to a smaller painting I'd never seen before.

"It's one of the last she finished," he said.

Ruth had painted roses, full blown, but with the lushness lost, the edges touched with a dark brown like the red of dried blood. Around the base of the blue bowl there was a mouldy softness of fallen petals. The painting glowed with a light like an approaching storm. It took my breath away. Took me right back to the garden on a day in early summer.

"Show me your favourite," she'd said. I'd been gushing over nodding flowers more numerous than the stars. I opened my arms as though to embrace the whole garden.

"No", she said, "I'm serious. I really want to know." Kneeling on the path, I touched a fingertip to the luminous blue of a forget-me-not and looked up at Ruth. "Perfect!" she said. "I could have guessed. Such a faithful little flower."

"Well, come on, Ruth," I coaxed. "Fair's fair. Let me guess your favourite." I cupped my hand around the gaudy petals of an oriental poppy. The scarf Ruth had used to tie back her hair that day—an exotic swirl of scarlet and orange and black—was the same one she'd wear a few weeks later to lunch with Karen. She flipped the end of it with a laugh like the clinking of the silver bracelets on her wrists.

"Well, maybe for today. But really, I love roses best."

And here were the roses. "Oh God, Steven, it's beautiful."

His lip twisted. "I hate it."

I missed Ruth so intensely in that moment I had to cover my face with my hands. If only she were here we would tiptoe into the living room, sit facing one another on the soft leather sofas and she would whisper, "He doesn't get it. He's too young. All he can see is dead flowers."

Ruth had never stripped her garden of fading flowers. She loved the carpet of petals. "Flowers are still flowers," she'd told me, "long after any notion we have of perfection is gone."

Steven walked away from me and faced the window and the brown stalks of the garden beyond. "Take it down and look at the back, Theresa."

I lifted the roses off the wall, turned to hold the back

220

so it caught the light from the lamp in the corner. *Roses for Karen*.

Ever so carefully, I rehung the painting. Stepped back because I was sure the petals would start to fall and I'd be buried, suffocated. I cleared my throat. "I think I'd like to have this one instead."

Steven turned around, arms at his sides. "She knew what she was doing when she put you in charge, Theresa. But I don't think it was fair that she asked you to carry her secrets around."

I crossed the room to a pair of wicker chairs where I'd sat so many times with Ruth, leaned with my elbows on my knees, my face in my hands. When I looked up he hadn't moved. "Which secrets are you talking about?"

"The baby secret. Gran told me I have a brother or sister out in the world somewhere. She said I needed to know this, because if this person ever got wind of an inheritance they'd turn up on the step and I should be ready to slam the door."

Everywhere I looked I saw Ruth's flowers. I was sure I caught a lingering whiff of her perfume in spite of the odour of solvents and paint in the room.

"Your grandmother probably meant well, Steven, but don't you think that's probably rumour? Your mom told me long ago that your dad's family never felt she was good enough for him."

Steven pulled out the other chair and sat down to face me. He took my hands and shook them gently. "It's not rumour, Theresa. And it wasn't news either. Dad told me about my sister a long time ago."

There was a rush to my face of blood, and heat and

tears. "Your mom didn't know that. If only she'd known that." I swallowed hard. "How old were you?"

He shrugged. "Sixteen maybe? He said Mom didn't want me to know, but he thought I had a right."

All of Ruth's secrets, her careful planning, swirled around me like flower petals in a windstorm. Grant's silence had not signified acquiescence. How could she not have known this, Ruth, who knew everything?

I squeezed Steven's hands. "Did he tell you she'd found your mom? That your mom met her? That I was with her?"

His eyes grew huge. "You know her?" He turned to look at the roses. "Her name is Karen, right?"

No, this was not Ruth's presence that was stifling me. It was Karen who was with us in the room, but just beyond reach. "Yes. Karen. Would you like to give her this painting? I have her phone number in my bag." My voice was beginning to break up. It would shatter with any more words.

Steven shook his head. "Not yet."

We stood at the window together and then Steven tapped lightly on the glass, turned to me with a slow smile. "I have an idea," he said.

In the flower bed outside the window, heavily thorned rose branches stretched away from the studio into the dusk. This close to the wall, and under the blanket of dead leaves, the dirt would still be soft.

He walked out of the room. I heard the door, and in a few minutes he was back with my jacket, and the white box.

Outside, the air was clean, and smelled only of snow.

This promised to be the first peaceful night in almost a year. There was no better place for Ruth.

A CRACK IN THE WALL

Marion closes the garage door, trudges across the lawn, and kicks half-heartedly at one of the posts on the For Sale sign. An army of real estate agents has trooped through her house today. She knew when she left for work this morning that they were coming. That the sign would be there. She steeled herself on the drive home. But the sight of her Tidal Wave petunias lapping at the feet of that death notice is too much.

When a car draws slowly to a stop across the street, she bends low over the cherry-coloured blossoms, trying to make herself invisible. She would retreat to the house except that Philomena bursts through the gate next door brandishing a piece of pipe. "Okay, let's get rid of that sucker. You want it down? I'll take it down."

"Not down. Moved. I want it out of the petunias."

Philomena crouches behind the sign, then springs up swinging. The sign buckles in the middle. One on either side, they haul up on the posts. They drag the sign across the lawn and lean it against the spruce tree. Philomena stands, hands on hips, shaking her head. "Now what the hell is this all about? I thought you guys were having a friendly divorce and you were staying in the house."

"Just until everything's sorted out. Time's up."

Philomena's arms enfold her. "Aw babe, we're gonna miss you. My fingers are crossed that the place doesn't sell. I hope you're asking the moon for it."

"I thought so." Marion nods toward the car on the street. "But apparently they're lining up already." She pats the shoulder of Philomena's purple sweatshirt and steps back. Her neighbour is all juicy curves, and smells as warm and sweet as a bowl of ripe plums. On a summer day years ago when Philomena was sunbathing in her backyard, hugely pregnant, Marion caught her son spying from his bedroom window with a pair of toy binoculars. Tim was young enough that he didn't register a bit of embarrassment. Just his usual wide-eyed "Wowzers!"

In the car across the road, two men and a blonde woman are talking and pointing.

Philomena nudges Marion with her elbow. "Want me to do something obscene so they'll go away? Remember, I get first right of refusal on new neighbours. I want to interview them before you sign anything."

From the corner of her eye, Marion can see the tangle of bikes on Philomena's lawn. Dennis wanted to wait until winter to list the house. The snow, he said, would hide Philomena's unkempt yard, and the boys were less likely to be outside. If a prospective buyer met even her five-year-old, the deal would be doomed. Out of loyalty to her neighbour, Marion protested, forgetting that she was the one who'd been stalling, hoping for one last summer in the garden. Dennis's eyebrows lifted. "Fine," he said, "we'll get on with it then."

And the realtor concurred. "Absolutely, a summer sale. The garden will sell the place."

She hoped things would move slowly, but there are these people in the car, and since she's been talking to Philomena, she's heard the faint but persistent ring of the phone inside the house.

Finally, the car eases away from the curb and Philomena flaps her hand like a little kid waving bye-bye.

"You found another place?"

Marion nods, the image of her next home suddenly comforting. "Close to downtown. The top floor of my cousin's house. I'll be fine."

"Is there a garden? Marion, I can't picture you living anywhere without flowers."

Her cousin's garden is the ultimate in low maintenance. Marion longs to hang baskets of fuchsia on the veranda, and arrange tubs of Martha Washington geraniums among the shrubs on the kidney-shaped islands of crushed shale. Perhaps next summer, if she and Connie are still friendly after such close proximity. For now, she'll fill the sunny upstairs kitchen window with potted gerbera daisies.

Marion imagines herself driving by her old house in dark glasses and a scarf next spring for a glimpse of the bed of mauve and pink tulips she planted the day before Tim died. Six years later, the bulbs should be old, diminished, and yet every year they come back more elegant and profuse than that first horrible spring.

Philomena shakes her head, wings of blue-black hair rivalling the gloss of the crows that have taken up residence in the blue spruce this summer. "I dunno about you and Dennis. You still driving out to the coast together for Jilly's wedding?"

"She's our daughter. Why wouldn't we?"

"Because you're getting a divorce, for crying out loud! You're supposed to hate each other's guts."

Marion bends to lace her fingers through a clump of chickweed that's insinuated itself into the mat of periwinkle. "If there was that much passion left in either of us, we'd still be married."

"Come in for coffee," Philomena says, looping her arm through Marion's.

In the kitchen, Philomena tips a pile of jackets off one chair, the cat off another. She pours coffee while Marion sits at a table littered with photos and scrapbook pages, stickers and borders. "New hobby," Philomena says. "I'm pasting all the cutesy stuff into books. Just to remind me, when I want to kill them, that I do love the little darlings."

When she lifts the steaming cup of dark roast coffee to her lips, Marion realizes she's still holding a handful of weeds. While Philomena rummages through the cupboards, Marion begins to arrange strips of stickers around the chickweed. Basketballs, skateboards, bikes, and puppies. A boy's life. The trappings that cluttered Tim's room. It's just as well she missed out on the scrapbook craze. She can't imagine opening such a book now.

"So who got to the 'fuck it' point first?"

"Hmmm?" Marion looks up.

Philomena has dropped into her chair, clutching a bag of cookies. She rips it open with her teeth and pulls out the plastic tray, passing Marion two Chips Ahoy before she answers. "You know that place where all the energy's used up? And you either say, 'fuck it' or you don't, and not saying it is even harder work." She leans on her elbows and regards Marion with eyes as strong and brown as the coffee.

Marion swallows a bite of cookie. "I'm not sure," she says. "Even though it was Dennis who moved out, I feel as though I've been gone for years."

Marion declines a second cup of coffee, and drifts across the lawn and into her own house.

The kitchen table is littered with realtors' business cards. The carpet she vacuumed before she left in the morning is as scuffed as sand after a beach party. She imagines ghosts of feet. Craters from the heavy soles of dress shoes, the blurry brush of stocking feet and the sharp circular imprint of high heels in a parade from the front door to the bedrooms and back out through the living room. A few ventured into the family room from the kitchen and all of those prints lead to the patio doors. She's sure they oohed and aahed over the back garden the way everyone does. Dennis set up the patio table and chairs, and for the first time in over a year that corner of the yard looks welcoming, lived in.

Marion can remember clearly the night they quit pretending. She picked fresh beans, and Dennis barbecued a fillet of salmon. He overcooked the fish, the edges curled, the flesh dry and bitter from too much lemon juice. They sat outside with the umbrella on the table tilted to shade them from the setting sun. Over coffee and fruit salad, Dennis folded the newspaper he was reading and leaned back in his chair.

"Marion, can you remember the last time we had sex?"

She swallowed a slice of woody-tasting nectarine without chewing, patted her lips with the paper serviette, then pushed the bowl away. "May twelfth." She would have preferred not to remember. All that day, she'd avoided looking at Dennis, knowing that his eyes would reflect her own black pain. They'd been in bed for hours when she realized that Dennis too was still awake, and that his back was quaking against hers. She turned and held him. Later, the comfort of their urgent lovemaking had allowed both of them to sleep. "Tim's birthday," she said. "May twelfth."

She thought for a moment that he'd reach across the table and take her hand, but instead he seemed to draw farther away. "And the time before that?" She shook her head. "That doesn't worry you?" he said.

She stared back at him, at the thin line of his lips, the twin creases of indecision between his eyebrows. The same look he would use to contemplate the Abraham Darby rose that has refused to bloom the last two seasons. "You're the one who's been sleeping in the den," she said. "I'm over my bronchitis. I don't cough at night anymore." She shrugged. "Come back."

He threw his arms over the sides of the chair and let them dangle, his chin slumped on his chest. When he finally looked up she could find nothing in his face.

"That's the whole point, Marion. I really don't care if I ever do. And you care even less."

The next morning he packed a small suitcase. He said he'd booked a week's holiday and was driving to Edmonton to visit his brother, then on to Jasper for a couple of days. He'd be in touch as soon as he got back.

For the first two days, Marion found herself wandering through the empty rooms arguing aloud with Dennis. "Well how would you expect people who've lost a child to behave?" And then, anticipating that he'd remind her that it had been six years, she'd say, "But it seems like yesterday. Doesn't it seem that way to you?" Knowing that the answer was yes. Finally she found herself agreeing with the dialogue she invented for Dennis. Agreeing that they acted as sad reminders to one another, and that they'd grown so far apart it was getting harder and harder to remember a time when anything they'd done together had brought them pleasure.

On the sixth day, she came home from work to find a U-haul out front and Dennis in the kitchen preparing supper. His closet was empty. His side of the bathroom vanity was bare. After they ate, they spent the evening deciding which pieces of furniture would best fit the small apartment he'd rented.

He was fussing over which lamp to take when she sat down on her half of the sectional couch and crossed her legs, tugging at the hem of her slacks. "Dennis, we don't have to do this. You can move into the den permanently and have the big bathroom for your own. I'll give you the living room and move my books and CDs to the family room. Why spend money on rent when we own a house?"

The words felt like a script she was required to deliver. She'd been trying all week to feel buoyant, to embrace the idea of a new start. And yet, in the back of her mind she'd carried the possibility that Dennis would have a change of heart somewhere between Jasper and the Columbia Ice Fields. Without either of them saying a word, they'd slip back into their old life and lump along wondering which of them would die first.

She was relieved when Dennis frowned and shook his head. "What would be the point of that?"

"It seems like a civilized kind of solution. I read about it in . . . oh, *Chatelaine* or somewhere." She tilted her head and squinted at him through the glare of the lamp he was still holding like a torch. "Unless there's another woman."

"No." He shook his head. "There never has been. You know that."

What he wanted most was to travel to corners of the world that made Marion hyperventilate at the very thought. He'd worked out a partial retirement and without the encumbrance of a house—and a wife, but he was tactful enough to refrain from saying so—he could spend at least six months of every year travelling.

"And what about you, Mare?" he said softly. "What will you do differently?"

When everything that came to mind seemed trivial, she waved her hand in what would have to pass as breezy relief. "Not a thing. But you see that's what will be different. I can do whatever I want without drawing a plan."

So far, it seemed that, apart from moving, nothing much would change. After she moved to the top floor of her cousin's house, she would greet the morning from a new window and drive a new route to her job at the bank. But she would spend her lunch hour on the same wooden bench in the indoor garden at the Devonian centre, and every evening she would curl up with a book on her pie-shaped chunk of the leather sofa.

And sometimes, if he wasn't in Milan sipping an espresso at a sidewalk cafe, she'd phone Dennis in his apartment on the other side of town to say goodnight.

In the midst of her inventing the conversation they'd have, the doorbell rings.

The man at the front of the trio has his arms spread wide as though he's going to embrace Marion when she opens the door. She steps back, but he continues to talk to the couple behind him, turning sideways now to include the front yard in the expansive gesture. "You'll never find a mature garden like this out in the new developments."

He beams at Marion, his face a mask of sincere friendliness, and hands her a card. "Mrs. Holland? I'm Gerry from Remax; these folks are Andrea and Kevin. They're in the market for a home in this area. I hope you don't mind that we didn't call first." These are the people who sat in the car watching Philomena relocate the For Sale sign. The woman's carefully tussled hair is more silver than blonde up close. About Marion's age. The age when people are scaling down, not buying family homes in the suburbs.

The man looks as though he's late for an appointment and as tightly wound as the spring on the screen door. He eyes the underside of the soffit where the paint is beginning to peel, then looks pointedly from Andrea's eyes to the roof. She shrugs. Marion holds the door open and stands uncertainly in the entrance to the living room.

"You just carry on with whatever you were doing, Mrs. Holland. Don't pay any attention to us."

She can't envision sitting in the living room like a piece of furniture while they discuss the condition of the carpet and the closet space, so she slips on her shoes and out the front door.

"Hey, Marion! Watch this!" One of Philomena's boys careens down his sidewalk on a skateboard, leaps into the air and executes a hair-raising turn into the street, then sweeps up Marion's driveway, missing the realtor's car by a breath.

"That's fantastic, Scotty. But be careful!"

He grins, looking exactly like his mother for a split second before he rattles off in the other direction. "I'm not Scott!" he shouts over his shoulder. "I'm Chris!" Of course he is. She's always known the boys by name. It's Dennis who calls them all Scotty.

She makes a slow circuit of the front yard. Dennis is coming to cut the grass again tomorrow night, and will remind her that, with luck, this will be the last mowing. Thinking she'll sit in the backyard, she opens the gate and comes face to face with Andrea. She's on the verge of retreating when the woman puts a hand on her arm. "I love your garden. Kevin's more interested in basements and plumbing, but I was so enchanted by the view from the kitchen window, I had to come out."

233

"Are you a gardener?" Marion asks. It's a test, really. Andrea's hand now rests light as a butterfly on the top rail of the fence. That flawless French manicure has never seen the inside of a gardening glove.

The woman shakes her head. "If only. I'd like to use time as an excuse, but it's really that I'm hopelessly ignorant." She points at the hanging baskets in the shady corner behind Marion. "Those are gorgeous. Perfect for that space. But I haven't a clue what they're called."

Marion turns to pinch a drooping head off one of the salmon coloured begonias, ignoring the bait. She promised Dennis she'd cooperate by keeping the house tidy, but she didn't agree to conduct tours, especially not tours of her garden.

"I adore roses," Andrea says and breezes across the deck and down into the sunken garden that was the last addition to the landscaping. Unfinished still after six years, but only Marion will ever know that the shale path was meant to be replaced with carefully arranged stone. Andrea crouches in front of one of the bushes. She balances with her fingertips, taking care that the knee of her linen slacks doesn't touch the dirt, and buries her nose in the crimson petals of Europeana. Marion could tell her that she's chosen one with little fragrance. That the English roses are the sweetest of all, but poor Abraham Darby, one of the few that Dennis chose, has been sending out blind tips for years. Probably best for the new owner of this garden to replace it with something bred for this climate. Morden Blush would bring the same brush of delicate pink and withstand the Calgary winter. Marion folds her arms and watches silently.

Finally Andrea stands, and dusts her hands together. "You don't remember me, do you?" she says.

Marion shakes her head.

"My daughter went to school with your son. Tom? I don't think she knew him well. But she was friends with the other boy, the one who was driving."

Marion can't answer. Even all these years later, there are times when she can't say his name aloud. Not the other boy's, nor Tim's.

"I understand there's a divorce. I'm sorry." Andrea takes a few steps toward Marion. "It must be hard for you to leave here, all the memories in this house."

The back door opens then and Kevin and the other man step out. "Absolutely not," the salesman says. "See how the ground slopes away? This area isn't prone to flooding, and this is one of the snuggest houses I've seen in a long time."

Marion bites her tongue. The well-patched crack in the laundry room wall is hidden behind shelves Dennis pounded up just last week. The past few summers have been dry, but for years they've held their breath through July and August, hoping they'd never have a repeat of the deluge that set everything but the piano afloat.

While Kevin once again draws Andrea's attention to the scabby paint, Marion slips into the house through the back door and down the stairs. If they've already seen the basement it's probably safe to hide there. But a minute later the door opens and Andrea's long beige legs appear on the other side of the iron stairway guard.

Marion slips into the dark storage cupboard under the stairs and quietly closes the door. This is where they've kept the small amount of liquor in the house since Tim's best friend played bartender to a gang of kids one day after school. He spotted the bottle of vodka in the kitchen cupboard, and the orange juice in the fridge and one thing led to another. When Jill finally came home and found her brother and three other twelve-year-olds drunk in the basement, she panicked and ran next door to enlist Philomena's help. By the time Marion arrived, the boys had all thrown up, been doused under a cold tap, and driven to their respective houses with strict orders to go straight to bed and plead flu. The kids chipped in a few days later and bought Philomena a bouquet of flowers. Marion leans against the wall and smiles. Will she be leaving the memories of Tim behind? No, he isn't in the house, or even under the basketball hoop that still hangs over the garage door. She'll carry him wherever she goes. Same way she's sure he'll travel with Dennis to the Great Wall of China.

Marion hears the sound of the back door opening, more feet on the landing. She holds her breath. How did this happen? Hiding in the dark in her own home?

"Never mind." Andrea's voice is impatient. "I don't need to see the basement. I want this house."

Marion waits until the footsteps overhead circle the rooms looking for her and then fade to the front door. A few minutes, then she tiptoes up the stairs and out the back door. She peeks around the side of the house hoping she'll see them driving away, but the car is still there with only Kevin in the back seat and the realtor behind the wheel. She swings round to the sound of heels crunching across the shale.

"I wanted one more walk though the roses," Andrea says. "I've driven by so many times and wondered if the backyard was as lovely as the front. And it is. Even more so."

"You live nearby?" Marion is baffled. Why are they looking at her house if they already live in the neighbourhood?

"No. When my first husband and I divorced we sold the house." She grimaces. "I hate the condo we're living in. I want a real house again. Kevin's not wild about the idea, but he'll come around."

Philomena's front door slams and Scott tears out. The real Scott this time. He's at the street before Philomena flies onto the step waving a piece of paper in one hand and a broom in the other. "This is the lost report card! Under your bed is not so bright, Scotty! You come back here, you little shit!"

Andrea throws her arms in the air, laughs. "Boy, does that bring back memories."

The man in the car is beckoning to her, but she turns to face the other way, tilting her head to look into the canopy of laurel leaf willow beyond the roses.

Marion doesn't remember hearing a last name in the introductions. "What's your daughter's name?" she asks.

"Lisa."

That's little help. It seems to her that half the girls Tim and Jill grew up with were named Lisa. "What's she doing these days? Still in school?" Tim would have graduated from university this spring. Engineering probably. Kinesiology. Philosophy. He had the brains and the motivation to accomplish anything he set his heart on.

Andrea continues to stare at the sky. "She never finished high school. I have a four-year-old grandson. I'm hoping she'll send him to live with me. With us. Here."

Then she turns and offers her hand. "Nice to meet you . . . "

"Marion."

The handshake is firm and honest, not languid as the manicure suggests. "Thanks, Marion. I love this house."

Marion hesitates. "The basement leaks, you know. Whenever there's a wet summer, that back wall weeps."

"Then we'll fix it. But thanks for telling me." She turns and strides to the car. The sun glints off her frosted hair. Marion watches them drive away.

"Takers?" Philomena leans on the fence, broom still in her hand.

"I hope so," Marion says. "I don't want to stay here for another killing frost." She opens the gate and walks into Philomena's arms.